"You Lo[...]"

he said. "I've never seen you look lovelier than you do now. A certain party, accustomed to having the limelight all to herself, won't welcome such formidable competition. The others are going to look at you and envy me."

"That's the most ridiculous thing I've ever heard. No one's going to envy you a thing. They'll look at my temper-flushed cheeks and know we've been quarrelling."

"On the contrary," he drawled. "They'll look at the sparkle in your eyes, couple it with your passion-flushed cheeks and think we've been making love."

Dear Reader:

I'd like to take this opportunity to thank you for all your support and encouragement of Silhouette Romances.

Many of you write in regularly, telling us what you like best about Silhouette, which authors are your favorites. This is a tremendous help to us as we strive to publish the best contemporary romances possible.

All the romances from Silhouette Books are for you, so enjoy this book and the many stories to come. I hope you'll continue to share your thoughts with us, and invite you to write to us at the address below:

Karen Solem
Editor-in-Chief
Silhouette Books
P.O. Box 769
New York, N.Y. 10019

DOROTHY VERNON
Edge of Paradise

Silhouette Romance
Published by Silhouette Books New York
America's Publisher of Contemporary Romance

Other Silhouette Books by Dorothy Vernon

Awaken the Heart
Kissed by Moonlight
Fire Under Snow
Sweet Bondage

 SILHOUETTE BOOKS, a Division of Simon & Schuster, Inc.
1230 Avenue of the Americas, New York, N.Y. 10020

ISBN: 0-671-57233-4

First Silhouette Books printing July, 1983

10 9 8 7 6 5 4 3 2 1

Map by Ray Lundgren

America's Publisher of Contemporary Romance

Printed in the U.S.A.

Edge of Paradise

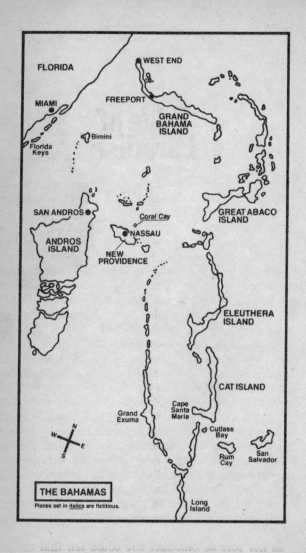

THE BAHAMAS

Places set in *italics* are fictitious.

Chapter One

The moment he entered the room her eyes fixed on him. Was it his commanding height that drew her gaze? Certainly he stood head and shoulders above the crowd, but that was secondary to some inner magnetism, a hint of wildness about him that was immediately apparent to her and that held her attention.

His hair was golden, burnished by a much hotter sun than ever warmed British shores, a conclusion that was heavily backed by his superb teak suntan. His perfect physique suggested that he was a doer rather than an observer. Not a backseat man, but a hands-on-the-controls man. The type who went looking for a challenge as opposed to one who merely accepted a challenge when it presented itself. An eye-on-the-highest-summit man who would scorn the easy path in favor of the difficult rock climb. The more forbidding the mountain, the greater the urge to conquer it; the more alien the river, the keener the desire to swim it.

Warming to her theorizing, she decided that his attitude toward women would follow the same pattern. An easy conquest would not fire his enthusiasm. The woman with the emotional strength to resist him would be the one he wanted to make love to. The thought merely served to increase her amusement at the situation.

In her role as onlooker she could tell that the two

beauties competing for his attention bored him with their eagerness. The redhead with her fingers curling hopefully in the crook of his arm and the well-formed blonde in the protective circle of his other arm were both exceptional lookers, but their enraptured delight at being with him, which almost amounted to gratitude, turned him off. Unless her judgment was very wrong, neither of these silly drooling females stood a chance with him. Couldn't they see what she could? Didn't they know that if they'd turned away, feigned disinterest, he would have been quick to follow?

Her own indifference wasn't feigned. He wasn't her type. If she was watching the tableau so avidly it was because she found it amusing, a bonus, because she hadn't expected to be so pleasantly entertained. She wasn't much of a party goer and had come to this one under duress. She disliked brittle social gossip almost as much as she disliked men who were too aware of themselves.

Just by looking at him, his stance, the arrogant tilt of his head, she could tell that he thought himself no end of an attraction. She must ask her hostess his name, out of curiosity, nothing more. It would be something to relate to Alison, Ally for short, who didn't have much of a social life these days. Ally's husband, Ray, had died over a year ago, leaving her with a tiny daughter, a large mortgage, an inflexible bank manager and, ultimately, a pressing need to find a job that would give her elastic hours and out-of-the-ordinary working conditions. Ally had come up with the perfect answer to her problem. As no boss would tolerate a toddler in his office, she had decided to be her own boss and open up a secretarial agency so that she could have Samantha with her all the time.

"Great!" Catherine had said, applauding her friend's initiative.

Ally had given her what could only be described as an old-fashioned look. "Ah, but wait until you've heard the snag. I want you to come in with me. I know it's a lot to ask. It will mean your giving up an absolutely fabulous, not to mention well-paid, job for the uncertainty of never knowing if there will be anything in the kitty at the end of the week to draw on, but I haven't the confidence, or the ability for that matter, to go it alone."

Catherine had replied cautiously. "Admittedly I'm good at my job, but I'm not exceptional."

She had loved her position as secretary to Charles Pemberton. She had believed him to be the best, the kindest, most considerate man she was ever likely to meet, and she had considered herself privileged to work for him and was naturally reluctant to give up this peach of a job to fall in with Ally's plan.

Weighed against this was the undeniable truth which Ally had next put forward. "If you won't, Cat, and I won't blame you if you say no, I'll just forget the whole thing." She had shrugged her shoulders and added philosophically, "I'll have to, for the simple reason that I don't know anyone else who would be stupid enough to join forces with me. Let's face it, I shall always put Samantha first, so my partner will have to tackle the brunt of the work, and should Samantha fall sick . . ." Her eyebrows lifted in explicit meaning.

"Your partner will have to shoulder the full burden," Catherine had said, finishing the sentence for her. She had to smile. Did she, after all, have a choice? She had then committed herself by adding, "How can I possibly say no to such an irresistible prospect?" As soon as Ally had finished gushing and thanking her she had continued, "We'll have to start looking 'round for premises in town."

"I already have," Ally had admitted impishly. "Well,

I knew you wouldn't let a little thing like a fabulous salary and a cushy job stand in the way of helping out an old friend, so I took an option on a place. Except that I should warn you, the word 'premises' is too grand to describe what I actually found."

The next day Catherine had dragged her feet and her sinking heart down a long, narrow passage between tall, overshadowing buildings, almost to the very end. She felt that it was the end when, finally, the key clutched in Ally's hand was fitted into a rusty lock. A door creaked open and, if it was possible, her heart sank even deeper into despair as she saw the condition of the room her friend was proposing to turn into their office.

"I know it's not much," Ally had apologized, "but places within our means aren't easy to find. A good scrub and a lick of paint should do wonders."

A lot of hard work was called for, but it wasn't really that which dulled her enthusiasm. "I'm not saying we couldn't bring this place up to scratch. We're neither of us afraid of bending our backs. It's the approach. It isn't what you'd call inviting. Will anyone trail all this way down to find us?"

"We'll have to see that they do. We'll think up some gimmick to make the public want to seek us out. It's because of where it is, down this long alley way, that it's cheap enough for us to afford it."

Even in her dismay, Catherine's sense of humor came to the rescue and found something to joke about in the situation. Latching on to the word "alley" she had said, "What will that make us? The alley cats!"

Ally was quick to pounce on the subtle combination of the nicknames they used for each other. The diminutives, Ally for Alison Black, changed to Butler on her marriage to Ray, and Cat for Catherine Mason, had been derived during their schooldays and had stuck.

"Cat, you're a genius!" Ally had exclaimed in delight. "That's it, the gimmick. That's what we'll call ourselves, the Allycats."

"I hope you're joking!" Catherine had gasped in response. "It's not dignified enough. It sounds positively—well—saucy. And that's a kind description."

"I know what it sounds like and I'm not joking. Dignity won't pay the bills. When we're established, when people find out just how efficient we are, we'll go respectable and change it to something sedate and businesslike, maybe 'Butler and Mason Typing Agency' if you're still feeling stuffy-minded. To begin with we *are* Allycats. We need something catchy to catch on. A name like that is sure to attract business and once people have tried us they'll see how reliable we are and they'll come back. It can't fail."

Well, that had been three months ago. It hadn't failed, but neither had the orders come rushing in with the speed which Ally had optimistically prophesied, and if the truth were to be admitted they were floundering badly.

The only reason Catherine had allowed herself to be roped into coming to this party was because the friend who was giving it had said that a writer would be among the guests, and he might want some typing done while he was over in England. As well as promising to be a well-paid commission, it could just be the springboard for future work. It was kind of Lois—her hostess—to think of her and make the meeting possible, Cat reflected.

Now, which man among this crowd was the writer? Was it the sweet-looking, nearly bald gentleman over there? He didn't look capable of writing racy detective novels which, according to her informative hostess, were the type of thing this fellow wrote. But then, you could never tell. Was it the tall, pale-faced, bespectacled, rather nice-looking man over there? He looked as if he might, but she still didn't think he was the one. While he was over in England, Lois had said. Catherine didn't discount him just because of his pale complexion. No matter how hot the sun got, some people never tanned. But the traveling gave them a certain kind of look, a polish, an assurance that came with the cosmopolitan lifestyle they led, which he seemed to lack.

She had partly done her homework. That is, once she discovered that there was a possibility of doing some work for him, she had trotted along to her favorite bookshop and bought his latest novel, but she hadn't had time to read more than a few pages. Although she wasn't as prepared as she would have liked to be, it wouldn't be an outright lie to say she had "read" him. It seemed cheeky to hope to take on a famous author's typing and not have read anything he'd written. He wrote under the name of Lucky Chance and Lois said his books hit the best-seller lists almost immediately and all but two of them had been made into movies.

She'd read enough to know that for his latest bestseller he'd chosen a warm climate, in keeping with the warmth of his dialogue, and a lush, exotic setting. There was an underlying something in his style that suggested that he would scorn library research and choose to live for a time in the place he intended to write about to soak up the local color. Again this was conjecture, but to her mind such a man wouldn't write anything he didn't have first-hand experience of. No matter how daring the episode he was plotting, before he put one word on paper he would go through the action himself.

After that, establishing his identity was as easy as counting up to three. All she had to find, and her eyes were already swinging 'round to locate him, was a challenge seeker with a superb suntan.

He just happened to be looking around at the same time. Oh, *no!* Of all the people in the room, the one person she would have to play up to was the one she'd taken an instant dislike to. For a moment their eyes locked. Hers, indicative of her thoughts, were furious and defiant. His reflected what was going on in his own mind, expressed speculation.

His eyes left hers to make a prolonged tour of her body; this, coupled with the feeling that had flashed across the room between them, left her in no doubt whatsoever as to the nature of his speculation.

She had received that sort of look from men before, and had perfected her own way of dealing with it. With ice, or ridicule, depending on which treatment she judged would be most effective. This time her brain seemed incapable of doing its normal thing. Instead of thinking, You should be so lucky! she sank low enough to wonder how she was shaping up.

Nature had blessed her with slim legs and a narrow waist, with nicely proportioned curves above and below, really quite modest in comparison with the voluptuous contours of his two companions, the blonde and the redhead, who were still fighting tenaciously for his escaping attention.

Natural poise came with the knowledge of having a good figure, but now, when she needed it more urgently than ever, Catherine's seemed to have deserted her. She wished she'd chosen a dress that didn't fit quite so neatly.

Having finished their inspection, his eyes lifted once more. They were a remarkable jade green in color, fringed with lashes that would have added an extra dimension of beauty to a woman's face, long, back-curling with golden tips, which still went perfectly with his indisputably male features. And they were signaling to her that he wanted to make love to her.

Inexperienced she might be, but she wasn't so juvenile that she couldn't recognize so clear a message. She had never felt so out of her depth, so divided in thought or so jangled in her entire life. The fact that she had always steered clear of the sort of danger he represented meant that she had nothing to draw guidance from to help her now.

Tapping some latent inner strength, she managed to compose herself sufficiently to give him the sort of quelling look that would have devastated most men. This one, after a moment of grave consideration, answered it with a smile, a smile that did precisely what it was intended to do: mock her feeble attempt to put him in his place and, as if that weren't bad enough, stir her interest.

In consequence her chin was the one to duck—in sick acknowledgment of the fact that she was not as immune to him as she would have wished. Had his smile flashed out on friendly impulse it would have been a different matter altogether. However, it was much too calculated to be sincere and the feeling she got was that if he hadn't been bored with his present company he wouldn't have exerted himself to look in her direction, and she wouldn't have been thrown into this state of contradiction.

Her dislike of his type had not wavered by the slightest degree, and yet over and over again she felt her eyes being compulsively drawn to his. She had never seen such compelling eyes in anyone, man or woman, ever before. They held her glance until the hot color flooded her cheeks, the cue for the sparkle of droll laughter to appear in their jade depths at this telltale sign of her inner confusion.

She was beginning to wish she had never come to the party, never subjected herself to this torment. He was playing with her emotions and even if he did condescend to give her some typing to do, he would be impossible to work for. Perhaps she should forget it and get out while she could.

But even as this thought crossed her mind he was firmly and not very gently disentangling himself from his female companions. Why? Did he mean to join her? She didn't wait to find out. She knew she had to escape and did so with all haste, to the bathroom, which was the one place he couldn't follow her. She asked herself if she weren't being just a little bit ridiculous, panicking at nothing.

She combed her hair, to little effect, as it did its own thing anyway. Dark copper in color, it was shiny and bouncy, held in some kind of check by its own weight, and reached below her shoulder blades. She retouched her makeup, scolded herself for not being better equipped to deal with the situation and felt, if not better, then certainly a little calmer.

She emerged from her hideout and returned to the overcrowded, overheated, intolerably noisy room. The party had livened up considerably during her absence. Someone had put on a record and couples were dancing. An arm snaked 'round her waist and she became engaged in a strenuous dance-cum-wrestling match with a man not much taller than herself. His one advantage was that he didn't block her view; as they circled the room her eyes could do likewise without being obvious. Where was he? She couldn't see him anywhere. Had he left?

Her partner swung her 'round and she came to a dizzy halt and fell, literally, into other arms. Finding the owner's face was merely a matter of raising the angle of her chin—and meeting the onslaught of mocking jade green eyes.

"Oh, you!" she said foolishly.

His hand on her back touched her nerves with

sensuous sweetness and she broke free of his dangerous hold. His jade eyes flicked over her, one brow lifting in amused awareness of the effect he had on her.

He said, "Do I take you home now? Or are you going to make me endure more of this exceedingly tedious party while we go through the formalities of getting to know one another first?"

"You're very sure of yourself," she began indignantly. Then, before she could put him in his place, an alabaster-white hand ending in long scarlet talons fixed predatorily on his shoulder.

A petulant voice said, "Darling, you've been an age. I thought you were getting me a drink."

"Of course, Ivy, my sweet. Come along and I'll drown you in it."

"My name is Poppy, not Ivy," the redhead cooed chastisingly, her red lips forming a beautiful pout.

His eyes rested on her clinging fingers. "I know. Ivy seemed more appropriate." Redirecting his gaze he said autocratically to Catherine, "This won't take long to deal with. Wait here."

As poor Poppy was dragged unceremoniously away to be dealt with, Catherine could find nothing to smile about in the ludicrous contrast between his indifference to Poppy and the taunting sweetness he was turning on her.

If he hadn't commanded her to wait in a tone that was heavy with meaning, it wouldn't have occurred to her to do otherwise. As it was, perversity made her move away. She circulated, and eventually came face to face with her hostess.

"Wonderful party, Lois."

"Glad you think so, darling. How lovely you look."

"So do you." Catherine came back on cue—and meant it. "In fact, you look ravishing."

The praise brought a gratified smile to her hostess's

lips as she asked with genuine interest, "How is the venture going? What is that absurd name you and Alison call yourselves? Ah, now I remember! Allycats!"

Catherine admitted, "We're not exactly living on cream. That's why . . ."

"I know, dear. I've had a word about you with my author friend," Lois said, inclining her head in his direction.

He had obviously dealt with Poppy and was now in conversation with the pale-faced man wearing spectacles. His features were strained with boredom. This was egomania in its most rampant form and her hackles rose in defense of that poor man.

"Like that, is it?" asked Lois, who was watching her face.

"Like what?"

"Snap judgment. You don't like him."

"No, I don't," Catherine declared vehemently. "He's too full of his own importance."

"Be fair, Catherine. He has achieved something to feel pretty special about."

"I know," she admitted with due remorse. "I feel awful talking about him like this when I'm hoping to get some work out of him. I'm not usually such a hypocrite."

"No–o, I'll go along with that. Neither are you usually such a bad judge of character, because take it from me, dear, he's quite charming. Perhaps you're in awe of him because he's acquired such fame. It affects some people that way. Anyway, to put you in the picture, I told him about Allycats and asked him if he could send some typing your way. I gave him your business address and he promised to get in touch. Now, must do my duty round. Have you all got drinks?" she said brightly, moving on to the nearest group of people.

Catherine realized that she'd forgotten to ask Lois his real name. No matter. She expected to encounter him again, and she did, by the simple expedient of turning 'round.

"Looking for me?" he inquired arrogantly.

So what if he knew she had been looking for him? He'd know why, because Lois had prepared the ground for her by mentioning the typing agency and informing him that she hoped he would give her some work to do. So she clasped her hands tightly, took a deep breath and said without preamble, "What do I call you? Lucky?"

His eyebrows lifted. "I hope so. You tell me."

Unsure of how to handle his blatant teasing, she tried again. "What's your name?"

"Paul Hebden," he replied after a slight pause, as if he thought she should have known it.

"I'm Catherine Mason. The Cat in Allycats. My partner Alison Butler is the Ally part."

He studied her face for a moment, the total absorption in his jade eyes replacing the cold boredom so recently contained there.

For the second time that evening she recognized the danger and knew she must not allow herself to feel flattered, no matter how novel it was to have the most interesting man in the room, the most interesting man she had ever met, come to that, looking at her as if she had suddenly changed from her average self into a creature of divine fascination.

"Mm," he said, in a way that made her wonder if he thought Cat was an appropriate name for her. She had been told more than once that her pointed face and sapphire blue eyes had a slightly feline look.

"Is this a new kind of party talk?" he said unexpectedly.

He was obviously telling her that he wasn't in the

mood to talk business. She sighed in resignation, and shivered despite the heat of the room. What he *was* in the mood for had been apparent all along.

He said, "Have you a coat to collect?"

She had hoped that her stay in the overheated smoky atmosphere wouldn't be too prolonged, but now she didn't want to leave its safety.

"If we go so soon, Lois will think her party is a flop."

"Don't be naive. It's doubtful that Lois will take note of our leaving in this scrum. But if she does, that's not what she will think at all."

She swallowed. She and Ally needed the work, but did they need it this badly? The simple answer was yes. So yes, she had a coat to fetch. And yes, he could take her home.

She hoped she knew what she was doing. On the way home, sitting beside him in his car, a very expensive model with long racy lines, her thoughts were chaotic to say the least. Obviously he was dallying her along with the intention of eventually giving her some work to do. The million dollar question was, if he did, would she be able to cope? Bosses had long been noted for making passes. Even Charles, who had been almost perfect in every way—until the end—had tried it on at first. He'd accepted the fact that she didn't want to play office hanky-panky and had gone back into line. Charles had respected her, going as far as to take her out on several occasions after his unsuccessful try-on, and every time his behavior had been that of a perfect gentleman.

But Paul wasn't Charles, as she was soon to find out. When she said, "That's where I live," he drove straight past, beyond the illuminating glow of the street lamp, and didn't stop until he found a place of deep shadows.

Even though she expected it, it still came as a shock to be crushed so forcefully against his chest as he imprisoned her mouth in a kiss that blotted out everything but the most intense spurt of pleasure she had ever known. Every other kiss she had ever received faded into insignificance before the impact of this new experience, one which showed the others up for what they were: icing sugar kisses, sweet but impotent, leaving her senses untouched.

Just as her mouth had softened under the skillful persuasion of his, so did her body soften to his touch as his fingers brushed against her in delicate introduction as he reached for the lever that lowered her seat. The maneuver was effected so smoothly that she didn't realize what was happening until the vulnerability of her reclining position struck her.

"No!" she gasped, struggling to sit up, a fresh wave of knowledge sweeping over her to increase her sense of panic.

Charles had been easy to repulse because she had wanted to repulse him. The recoiling of her flesh had been a blow to his pride and he had backed away from that as much as from her frosty, affronted protest.

But what man would listen when her body was giving out a different kind of message? He would take his cue from the exhilarated wildness of her pulse, the vibrating tingle of flesh that felt as though it must surely melt under the heat of its own response.

She had always prided herself on having a high sense of self-preservation and had guarded against the obvious harmful addictions such as cigarettes and alcohol, not realizing that it was easy to refrain from smoking when you found the taste of tobacco unpleasant. She quite enjoyed the occasional glass of wine, but hard liquor had little appeal for her.

Paul Hebden, though, could easily get into her blood. If she were foolish enough to let this happen, she would run the risk of never getting him out of her system again. He spelled danger for her. Resisting him would be the hardest test of stamina she had ever faced or was likely to come up against in her entire life. Despite all the confusion he wrought in her, her mind was surprisingly clear on that point.

Her next piece of action was a masterful cover-up of the battle she was fighting. "I'm getting out of this car, Paul, and don't try to stop me."

"I never need to exert physical strength over a woman," he said, his tone implying that it was naive of her to think he ever needed to resort to such measures. Women would always be readily available to him.

In one smooth operation she was released from his arms and her seat was brought back to its original upright position.

"Don't call me, I'll call you," she said, her dark copper hair swinging defiantly as she got out of his car. Even to her own ears her words sounded like a line from an old movie.

"Do that," he instructed urbanely. "Seven-thirty tomorrow. The Park Royal Hotel. Call *for* me. If you're not there on the dot, I won't wait. But you'll be there."

"You reckon? I'm afraid your confidence is in for a knock." Her quick breathing might tell him she was off balance, but her voice was as composed as she could have wished.

His smile mocked her. He didn't say anything; he didn't need to. He knew as well as she did the effort it took her to walk away.

Chapter Two

Sleep was not to be wooed. After restlessly tossing and turning for thirty minutes or so, and still not being able to get the wretched man out of her mind, she put on the light and reached for her bedside reading matter. She had quite forgotten that the book she'd left handy was the one she had recently purchased—*his*.

Was there no escaping him?

She opened the book. Might as well find out if she found his writing style as disturbing as she found him. As she had only read the first few pages, she started again at the beginning, and as before, she was immediately absorbed. He was clever with words, and devious. She discovered meanings now that she had missed the first time and before she got to the bottom of the third page a blush rose to her cheeks, one which was to renew itself every few pages. Yet she was full of admiration for his writing technique. She knew why he had such a large and faithful readership. His characters were flesh and blood; every word he wrote stood out with sparkling clarity, justifying its existence, which was to further the plot. No boring padding, and even the bits that made her blush, the sex passages, although too earthy for her taste, were no worse than one would expect in a hard-hitting, no-punches-pulled novel obviously aimed at a masculine market.

Despite that—or because of it—she was adamant on

one point. No matter how good the pay was, or how desperately she and Ally needed the money to keep Allycats afloat, she couldn't work for him. If this novel was representative of the stuff he wrote, she wouldn't be happy taking on his typing.

He wrote with obvious enjoyment and gusto, and she could just imagine him sitting a few feet away from her desk, his sardonic jade eyes following her progress as she typed out his manuscript. She could see it all so clearly in her mind's eye—his mouth curling in knowledgeable derision, anticipating the exact moment her fingers would stumble on the typewriter keys as the red awareness flooded her cheeks. All her prudish instincts came rushing to the fore. She couldn't do it, not even for Ally's sake!

Usually she was the first in to work, but the next morning she didn't need to take her key out of her purse. The door was unlocked, Samantha was occupied with her toy bricks in the corner she'd claimed as her own, and Ally was sitting at her desk, fretting over the account books.

As Catherine entered, Ally's chin swung up and she leaned back against the padded upholstery, looking too small for the executive chair which they had picked up for a song and done up themselves.

Ally was small in stature, but in spirit she matched up to a giant, and it was this which had bullied Catherine and kept them both going when their backs were weary, when their raw-from-scrubbing fingers could barely hold a paintbrush and their noses and stomachs revolted at the smell of soap and paint. They had scrubbed and painted and carpeted and furnished. They'd hung Japanese prints on the newly painted walls and fixed a nameplate and a new, shiny brass doorknob on the newly painted door. And all this time it had been

Ally's indomitable spirit, her cheerful, cheeky bounce which had held them together.

Now, as she sat in that outsize chair, her wispy fringe sticking out where she'd pushed her fingers through it, the bubbling animation of her tiny-featured face subdued in dejection, even her spirit looked small.

It gave Catherine an enormous jolt to see her friend looking so down—so defeated. Ally was a fighter. She'd fought during the year of Ray's illness, keeping depression at bay and Ray's spirits up as well as her own, despite the fact that she had just found out that she was pregnant with Samantha when Ray's listlessness was diagnosed as a blood disorder.

The knowledge that nothing could be done for him had been an extra burden to carry on her slight shoulders. She had always been the strong one in the marriage, the one to keep an eye on the finances and make the major decisions. After much soul-searching she had made her hardest decision: She thought it best not to tell Ray until almost the end, when it would be impossible to keep it from him any longer. He was charming, but weak, showing a marked tendency to crumble in a crisis, and he became querulous if he thought he was being given a bad deal. She knew this and loved him not a whit less because of it. She tried to explain to his parents that she was afraid that if he was told he would withdraw from the harshness of the sentence into a secret shell of his own, where they wouldn't be able to reach him. They pooh-poohed the idea, not seeing their son through her realistic eyes, and insisted that he had the strength of character and the *right* to know. Ally fought bitterly with them on the issue, forfeiting any hope of receiving help and support from them afterward. Her reward was the knowledge that the last year of her husband's life was the happiest he had ever known. To this end she had spent money as if there were no tomorrow for either of them, at bitter cost to her own solvency afterward. His parents couldn't see that she was acting with loving unselfishness. They would have had her make their son miserable with her tears, and condemned her laughter and cheerful disposition as outrageous, and made it clear that they wanted nothing more to do with such a heartless, uncaring creature.

So it came as something of a shock to Catherine to hear Ally's reply in answer to her urgent query of what was wrong. "Ray's parents came to see me last night."

"And?"

"They want to take responsibility for Samantha."

"Take Samantha away from you, you mean?" Catherine said bluntly.

"Yes."

"And leave you with nothing. Don't they think you've suffered enough?"

"That's the whole point, they don't think I've suffered at all. So I did go a bit mad with the spending at the end. There was such a lot of living to cram into that one year. But they won't see that before then I was the one to curb Ray's extravagance. They think I should have conserved what little savings we had to provide for Samantha after Ray's death. In not doing so, I've acted irresponsibly and proved myself a totally unfit mother for their grandchild, or so they say, and they're graciously offering to take her off my hands. It's their view that if I can't take care of my own affairs, how can I possibly take care of my child?" A flicker of fierce anger came to her eyes at the injustice of it, which just as quickly extinguished itself in despair. "Perhaps they're right," she said, giving the account books a shove in Catherine's direction. "I hate to admit it, but

I'm not the businesswoman I thought I was. I've not only conned you, I've conned myself as well. Perhaps it might be as well to get out while there are still some assets to split between us and not a pile of debts. I'm sure that Charles would give you your job back if you asked him."

If she crawled, perhaps he would. If she went back to him in all humbleness and admitted that he had been right in the things he had said, that she *had* repaid all the kindness he had shown her with ingratitude.

Charles had been a big letdown. She had expected him to applaud her actions, find something worthy in her wanting to go to the aid of a friend and perhaps even do something constructive to help put the venture on its feet. Instead he had accused her of using him. Certainly he had helped her in her job and she was grateful to him for having sufficient faith in her initially to think she could do it. She would be the first to admit that she couldn't have managed without his guidance— but she had always given him a loyal day's work and it was pathetic of him to moan that he'd got used to her and accuse her of leaving him in the lurch.

She hadn't told Ally any of this, even though she knew that her friend had been puzzled that the break between her and Charles had been so final. Ally had assumed that they would continue to see each other, a thought which had also crossed Catherine's mind. There had been a time when she thought that something more permanent would come out of their casual dating. She shivered, as though suddenly realizing what a lucky escape she'd had. And anyway . . .

"Allycats is surely a success," she protested. "You said yourself only the other day that we were getting a fair number of orders for work coming in."

"True. But I made two bad miscalculations. We've

done this place up practically for nothing, but we've still had to pay money out for essentials, typewriters and suchlike. Telephone installation and the advertising we've had to do haven't come cheap. We're in a wobbly position now because I didn't have any savings to put in and yours—and I'll never be able to thank you enough for investing your own money—didn't add up to enough working capital. That was my first miscalculation."

"And the second?"

"Me again. It never occurred to me that I wouldn't be able to take up from where I left off before I gave up work when I was expecting Samantha. I'm rusty. It's going to take awhile to pick up my speed and get my pre-Samantha efficiency back. I'm not pulling my weight. Whatever happens, I want you to know that I don't regret trying. Even though it seems that we've fallen on our faces, I'm glad we had a go. If nothing else, it's shown me what a true friend you are. I'll never forget what you did for me."

"Will you please stop this! This halo is giving me a headache. And anyway, all the favors aren't on one side. What did I give up? A job I was feeling too complacent about, which is the next thing to boredom. A man who wasn't as nice as I thought he was. No, *I* should be thanking *you*, Ally."

"You're not just saying this to make me feel less guilty?"

"I promise you I'm not."

But for Ally she would have gone on working for Charles, possibly drifted into a deeper relationship with him, which would have fulfilled her only because she didn't know any better. She would never have gone to that party in the hope of finding work, never met Paul, never been awakened by his kiss. Even as her lips

tingled at the memory, they curved in a smile of
inspiration. She could use Paul as a lever to make Ally
change her mind.

"I haven't had a chance to tell you about my meeting
with the writer at Lois's party last night."

"You actually got to talk to him. Lucky you!"

"No." Catherine couldn't resist it. "Lucky Chance."

"Oh, you!" Ally said, pretending to throw her
stapler at her, before asking with betraying eagerness,
"Did he say we could do some typing for him? He's
very prolific, turns out books at an amazing rate. If we
got in with him on a regular basis it would set us up
nicely."

"I'm seeing him at his hotel this evening."

"To discuss working for him? He did mention that
specifically?"

"What other reason could he have?" Catherine
inquired casually.

That seemed to placate Ally, and Catherine was glad
she hadn't been called upon to give a proper answer to
her friend's question. When Paul had asked—no
commanded—her to go 'round to his hotel that evening,
the typing of his manuscript had not been the upper-
most thing on his mind.

"What's he like?" Ally asked. "Nothing like his
books, I'll bet."

Catherine felt that a certain amount of caution was
required here. "Have you read any of his books?" she
asked carefully.

She had changed her mind about doing his typing for
Ally's sake. If it would provide the means to allow Ally
to keep Samantha instead of letting her late husband's
parents gain control, then she wasn't going to balk at
what she had to do. At the same time, she thought that
Ally might share her delicacy of feeling when it came to
typing such racy material, so it seemed a good policy to

let the torrid shock come later. She should have known better.

Ally scoffed. "You're being stuffy again. Read any of his books, you say? I've read all of them! I'm his greatest fan. I like having my toes curled up. You shock too easily." Reacting to the look on Catherine's face she stopped scolding and said kindly, "There's nothing to be scared about, you know. Writers are never like what they write."

"This one is," Catherine affirmed emphatically. "He thinks he's God's gift. He probably bases all his heroes on himself. You know the type—lives in the place he's writing about and samples the action first hand."

"Is he married?"

"I don't know." A beginning frown was already making its presence known on her brow when she remembered how perceptive her friend was. It had never even occurred to her that he might be married until Ally put the thought there. She quickly rearranged her features and injected indifferent laughter into her tone. "I don't think he is. I shouldn't imagine the woman's been born who would put up with him on a permanent basis."

"I was just going to say that I should hate to be his wife, if your judgment is correct. So I'll amend that to girlfriend." Perhaps her indifferent act hadn't been as successful as she had hoped, because Ally got in sneakily, "You haven't got aspirations in that direction, have you?"

"Of course not. I know exactly what you're getting at. It would be highly unpleasant to wonder, in the tender moments, if your lover was researching a love scene for his next book. Don't worry about me. It's a business proposition and that's the way it's going to stay."

"What if he wants you to go with him?"

"Go *where* with him?"

"Wherever he's going to set his next book. I was just thinking," Ally said with a mischievous giggle. "I hope it's not a whaler in the Antarctic."

"Do you mind!" Catherine could think up enough disquieting thoughts off her own bat without Ally's dubious help.

This conversation with her friend strengthened her resolve that the meeting with Paul Hebden at his hotel must be conducted on a strict business footing, and that meant putting the seduction of her favorite deep claret-red dress, so becoming to her dark hair, back in her wardrobe and selecting the protective veneer of a dress made of less clingy material, its color the dense gray of woodsmoke. For her peace of mind it was lucky she didn't realize what an illusory protection it was. The cut of the dress, with its own matching jacket, was excellent. Her assessment that it was the type of outfit the retiring companion of a high-born lady would wear to keep her place in the background was spot on, but she failed to see that her own looks foiled any attempt to appear insignificant. If anything, the severity of its color and cut enhanced the sweetness of line from her forehead to chin, the tender grace of her throat and youthful curves. If the question of her age cropped up, people were always surprised to learn that she was twenty-two, because she looked much younger, possibly because of the childish hugeness of her brilliant sapphire blue eyes within the silky frame of her hair.

She reached for her ivory-backed hairbrush, which was part of a set given to her by her mother on her sixteenth birthday, and applied several vigorous strokes. It was the last birthday present she had ever received from her. One murky night, in a moment of carelessness, her mother had stepped off the pavement, and the driver of an oncoming car hadn't been able to apply his brakes soon enough to offset the dangerous condition of the rain-polished road surface. Her father had subsequently remarried, choosing for his bride a widow with two young children. He had decided on a fresh start and had made a home for himself and his new family in the West Country, a place without memories. Most of the time Catherine could use her hairbrush without getting a lump in her throat. But now wasn't one of those times and a poignant sadness made swallowing difficult. "Don't you dare go soft on me," she scolded herself aloud as she reached for her jacket.

The Park Royal Hotel had a very imposing facade. As Catherine walked toward it, the commissionaire, his dark uniform resplendent with gold braid, raised a white-gloved hand in a military salute before darting ahead to open the door for her.

She could have done without the red-carpet treatment; she felt overawed enough at the prospect facing her. She wished she hadn't been so brusque with Paul Hebden, a little less dogmatic that she wouldn't keep the appointment. She sighed. It had been an instinctive reaction, and no way could she have foreseen the possibility of her having to eat humble pie.

From her superior height the girl at the reception desk seemed to look a long way down her nose at Catherine. It was a slightly aquiline but very elegant nose, which suited the elegance and haughtiness of her face. Cool blondes seemed able to look haughty without trying, an ability which Catherine envied at that moment.

It was quite amusing to see how dramatically the other woman's expression altered when Catherine gave her name and asked for Mr. Paul Hebden.

Envy was now written all over the receptionist's face

and her tone was positively fawning as she cooed, "Mr. Hebden left instructions that you were to go straight up to his suite, Miss Mason."

It was an odd sensation to be eyed up and down by a girl who, in Catherine's opinion, was ten times better looking than she was and know that the girl was wondering how she had pulled it off. She wanted to say, "It's not like that at all. It's for a job, so puzzle no more." Even more than that she wanted to turn around and go home. Dull, safe, not-very-nice Charles suddenly seemed a much more desirable prospect than the golden tiger man sitting upstairs in wait to gobble her up.

She took note of the number of his suite and marched toward the lift, saying under her breath, "You just try it, boy. You might find yourself with a bad case of indigestion."

She had to knock three times before his deep voice instructed her to enter. Admittedly, a mouse could have done better than her first two attempts. She wondered if she'd exaggerated his virile attractiveness in her mind, imagination running riot and all that.

He came forward to greet her, a sardonic twist to his mouth. A white silk figure-molding shirt was tucked into the dark trousers of his formal suit. The jacket, obviously in readiness to slip on, was laid across the back of a chair. From his arrogant golden head, down his well-toned body, which suggested a disciplined, healthy lifestyle and physical strength, to his polished black shoes, he exuded an expensive and immaculate gloss. Her eyes returned to renew their acquaintance with his face, taking pleasure in the strong features, the well-shaped masculine mouth, the obdurate quality—a definite character clue—of his thrust-out chin. Saving the best for last, she dwelt finally on those splendid jade green eyes. No, imagination hadn't run riot. If anything, her memory had sold him short. He was even better looking than she had remembered.

The amused awareness in his eyes, a look that had been maintained for several seconds, belatedly penetrated her brain, causing her to dip her chin in dismay and anger at allowing herself to be caught studying him so intently. What could she have been thinking of? Her consternation invited his smile. She heard it in the hateful smugness of his tone and saw it curling the corners of his mouth as her eyes dropped away.

"I told you that you would come," he said.

"So you did. You apparently knew more than I did," she said, flaunting her chin at him again.

"May I ask what made you change your mind?"

"Necessity."

"Necessity?" he repeated, showing his annoyance at her tendency to throw him by saying the unexpected thing. "Is it your special gimmick? Or is it a new trend? If so, let's hope it soon drops from fashion."

"What trend?"

"This way you have of talking in riddles. Shall we discuss it over dinner?" he asked, his bland smile returning as he reached for his jacket and slid his arms into it, as though the matter were settled.

Standing firm, not only against him but against the rumbling of her stomach reminding her that she had been too tensed up to eat before she came, she said, "I'm not dressed for the kind of place you obviously have in mind."

He awarded her a brief summing up look, showing no sign of perturbation, although he must have seen that her plain dress was ludicrous beside his formal attire. His tone was pleasantly persuasive as he said, "You look all right to me."

She gulped. He hadn't used his writer's craft to pay her a flowery compliment. He had really sounded as though he meant it. Yet she went on, just as if he hadn't spoken, "In any case, dinner isn't a good idea."

His eyes lowered again, and this time the kindly look was more prolonged and stayed below the level of her chin. "You can't be dieting. You've got an excellent figure. Unless it's that way because you watch your diet?" he asked as an amused afterthought.

"I can eat what I like. I'm this way naturally," she said, wishing he'd raise his eyes and at the same time hoping he wouldn't because she didn't want him to look at her face, which she was sure showed her flustered thoughts.

"If that isn't the reason, what is? I thought . . ." His forehead furrowed in puzzlement. "Our communication system is decidedly erratic. Would you explain what you mean?"

"There's nothing to explain," she said shortly. "You don't have to take me out for a meal; in fact, I'd prefer it if you didn't. I would like to keep this on a strictly business footing."

"Business footing?" he repeated. "I'm not with you."

"Allycats. You can't have forgotten," she said in dismay.

He acknowledged, "I do recall your mentioning something about it at the party. I remember thinking what a very pretty name you have—Catherine—and how sinful it was to let anyone shorten it to Cat, besides being totally inappropriate." Her wish to know what he thought *was* appropriate was on the point of being granted even as she worked to banish it, because such curiosity was treacherous. "Would you like to know what pet name I would prefer to call you by?"

"No," she said in defiance of her own softening attitude.

"Then I won't tell you," he said tantalizingly.

"I do believe you're doing this on purpose," she burst out in fury. "You're finding it fun to taunt me." Her mind, which was going 'round like a revolving door, admitted a new thought: If you weren't interested, why did you ask me to come here tonight? Her thoughts changed course again and she said with renewed indignation, "Unless you've had second thoughts—in which case the decent thing would have been to tell me straight out instead of leading me on like this."

"Obviously that's not the case. Would I still want to take you out for a meal if I'd changed my mind?"

"I don't know. You might—to let me down lightly."

"Now why should I want to do that?"

"You might think I'm inexperienced."

His brows came down. "I'm not sure I like the meaning of that."

"I can't see anything to take exception to. I can understand that you might want to deal with someone . . . well . . . established. But have you thought that the fact that we're new brooms could be a point in our favor? In the matter of building up good will it's imperative to give efficient, satisfactory service."

She was conscious of a change in his manner. It might be her imagination, but he seemed a different person than the man who said he thought her name was pretty and told her in all sincerity that she looked all right to him.

No, it wasn't her imagination. He had dropped that teasing smile which had brought the blushes to her cheeks and his attitude had turned colder—icy, even. She didn't know the reason for his rapid personality change and could only stare at him dumbfounded as she tried to puzzle it out.

But what was there to puzzle out? Wasn't it obvious? He was angry because she was refusing to let him wine and dine her. Feminine adoration had ruined him. He was so used to getting his own way with women that when one stood up to him he didn't know how to cope.

If the only way she could get his business was by being "nice" to him, she didn't want to know. Let him get his typing done by a more accommodating girl, if that's what he wanted. She wasn't going to lower her principles and be blackmailed into anything, even if it did mean the end of Allycats.

"Apparently we have nothing to discuss, Mr. Hebden. So if you will kindly excuse me, I'll say goodnight."

"Don't be so hasty," he remonstrated sharply. "I didn't understand. Now, sit down and let's talk this out. And you can cut out the high-handedness. In the circumstances it's downright ridiculous."

She was too taken aback to do anything else but comply, but not without a tiny surge of gratitude, because it went against the grain to have to beg for work, and her legs were beginning to shake under the pressure. She didn't think they would have supported her for much longer.

"I suppose the situation isn't all that unusual," he said after a moment of brooding contemplation.

She felt instant sympathy for him. "You must be heartily sick of being approached in this fashion," she said. Because obviously that was why he was annoyed. She saw now that he would be a ready target. Typing the manuscripts of such a celebrated author would carry an enormous amount of prestige. Not to mention being the first to read his work, before his publisher and his public.

The look he gave her was wry. "I've been approached in this way before. Yes, I'll admit to that. The difference is that I've always been aware of it before.

What an extraordinary girl you are. I don't know what to make of you. Just as a matter of interest, how did you get involved in this racket?"

"It was Ally's idea. Her husband died and left her financially insecure. He was ill for a year. He didn't know he was going to die, although Ally did. She thought it better to use their savings to cram a lifetime of all the good things he wouldn't have time to do into one fabulous year, and worry about the consequences of keeping a roof over her head and taking care of Samantha, their daughter, afterward."

"Mm."

"What's that supposed to mean?"

"I was just wondering what you are. A soft touch or a fool."

She was instantly on the defensive. "Ally didn't twist my arm. I left my secretarial job of my own free will to go in with her, though I was thinking mostly of Ally and little Samantha at the time. The partnership has given her the flexible hours she wouldn't find in a nine to five office job, and I don't regret it. It's opened my eyes to a lot of things. Ally says it's shown her who her friends are, and the same applies to me. It's shown me who *my* friends are, too."

"I can imagine," he said tersely. "How old are you?"

"Twenty-two."

"Have you any family?"

"My father . . . and I suppose I should also say a stepmother, stepsister and stepbrother, but I don't really know them at all," she said revealingly.

"I see." A pause. "If I take you on, you understand that I won't share you with anyone. That will be a condition. Naturally, the price will match it."

"That will be all right. Ally can deal with the other business."

His face was oddly without expression. "I'm flying

out to the sun tomorrow. To the Bahamas. How does that sound to you?"

"You mean you want me to come with you?"

Ally had said he might want to take her with him to work on his next book, but although the possibility had registered in her mind she hadn't really believed that it would materialize.

A girl she'd been at school with had trained as a nanny and she had got herself a job looking after the children of a Greek shipping magnate who was a millionaire many times over. Life was now one permanent holiday for her. Apart from being fabulously well paid—she earned as much in a month as Catherine had earned in a year while working for Charles—the family spent their vacations in the world's most publicized play spots, and naturally she went with them.

It had always been Catherine's dream to travel, and her savings, which she had used without a qualm to set up Allycats, had been earmarked for that purpose. She couldn't believe that her objective was going to be realized. This sort of thing happened to other people, never to her.

In view of all the joy singing in her head, how very banal she sounded as she solemnly nodded and said quietly, "The Bahamas sound good to me."

Chapter Three

"But . . . tomorrow? You did say we'd be going tomorrow? That doesn't give me much time. How long will I be away for?"

"Depends. For the moment I would prefer to keep that part open."

"I understand. If I'm not up to scratch, I may find myself packed back home in under a week. Well, that's fair enough."

"It could work the other way. I might just decide to keep you on a permanent basis."

"Yes, I suppose there's always that possibility," she said, sounding brighter. "Would you like to try me out now?"

She'd had the foresight to tuck her shorthand pad into her handbag in case he wanted to test her speed and she assumed that a portable typewriter would be a vital part of his luggage and easily accessible if he wanted to see her typing skills. Anticipating his affirmative reply, she began to unbutton her jacket, feeling that she would be more comfortable, and therefore more efficient, without its hampering presence.

A funny, strangled sound emerged from his throat as he stretched out his hands and firmly buttoned her jacket back up. "That won't be necessary."

She didn't know what brought the blush to her

cheeks, his peremptory tone or his fingers performing the intimate task in the proximity of her breast.

"I was looking at it from your point of view," she said in an unnaturally sharp voice, which etched his frown into deeper lines of disapproval. If he wanted a puppet assistant who never answered back he ought to steer clear of the personal touch, dictate straight into a machine and send his material through the post to be typed.

"And here I was thinking I'd thwarted your desire to display your talents to me," he drawled.

She couldn't understand the scoffing inflection in his voice, but it was instinctive to retaliate. "I thought that ten minutes now would save you the cost of my fare if I didn't match up to your expectations."

He was a long time in replying. When he did his tone was overlaid with sarcasm. "Have you any reason to suppose that you won't match up to my . . . expectations?"

"No," she said, puzzled and disturbed by the studied pause and his manner in general.

"And do you really think you can do full justice to your talents in ten minutes?"

For some totally unknown reason she found herself twisting her fingers into her hair, as if there were something improper about the question.

Nor could she know—because it wasn't apparent in his manner—how unnerving he found those candid eyes viewing him in judgment. He met her gaze steadily, but there was no flinching away, no flicker of anything in those clear sapphire depths, and still no reply on that uncompromisingly straight mouth.

"Well, blast it, can you?" he demanded.

Her eyelids fluttered, her glance dropped, but she quickly looked up again to say, "No, I don't imagine so."

"There's your answer then," he said savagely. "I'll just have to take you on a 'goods on approval' basis."

The rush of words, an instantaneous reaction, came crisply to her lips. "Are you trying to insult me?"

"I doubt if that would be possible."

He was back in fighting form again, his equilibrium restored by the loss of hers. Before her mind could grind into action again he strode away from her, searching for pen and check book and a flat surface on which to write.

Provoked beyond endurance, seething passionately, she thought, I'm a fool to wait. If I'd any sense I'd get up and walk out that door. The man's unbalanced. He must be. And I must be, too. Because she seemed incapable of following her own wise counsel. If she got up now, if she walked out that door, there would be no turning back and she would be walking out of his life for good. She couldn't do it.

She hung her head in shame and humiliation at this admission of cowardice. She was curious to know him better, and cowardly because she suspected that if she attempted to escape, he would drag her back.

She sensed that he had adopted a certain proprietorial attitude toward her. She didn't know why this should be; it made no more sense than anything else in this decidedly bizarre set-up did. For some incomprehensible reason he had taken it upon himself to be responsible for her. In place of her errant father? No! Most definitely not! He wasn't old enough to be her father.

She wasn't sure of his age. He could slot in anywhere between the thirty and thirty-five marks. And he certainly didn't look at her in the way a father would.

How *did* he look at her? The complexity of the man made that question difficult to answer. When she had first arrived his look had been one of intense desire. He had been all charm, chasing her like mad so that she had wondered, in a panic of reciprocal desire and doubt, how she could work for him and not be hounded straight into his bed. Then, abruptly, all that had changed and it seemed as though he wanted no physical contact with her. It was very odd. He had viewed her with distaste, but not with actual dislike, if that were possible. There might be something about her that didn't appeal to him, but there was more about her that did. He was fighting himself, attracted to her in spite of himself. It was either that, or it was all a big bluff. Could that be it? Was he pretending uninterest, aversion even, because he thought it would make her feel safe, and then when he'd lured her away, beyond the protection of home surroundings and familiar things, would he drop the pretense and start chasing her again?

These thoughts were better left alone. If she admitted to the possibility that he had designs on anything other than her shorthand and typing skills, then she would have to say she'd changed her mind and ask him to tear up the check. She didn't want to do that. Not solely for altruistic reasons, because if Allycats was to survive it needed a quick injection of cash, but also because the tearing up of the check would end the matter and there would be no reason for further contact between them.

Paul returned to tower above her, his aggressive stance matching the set of his chin. She still had no idea what she had done to earn his mockery and contempt. She did know that her thoughts on his not-so-innocent designs on her body were too recent not to tinge her cheeks a bright guilt-pink, and wondered what he was making of that. It probably added strength to whatever malformed notion he'd got into his head about her.

As he looked down at her his mouth moved into a deeper smile of bitter contempt, increasing her uneasiness and, to her further consternation, causing her blush to intensify. Charming! She was behaving as though she had something to be ashamed of.

"Here," he said, thrusting the check at her. "That should do for a start. There'll be more later if you're still with me."

Puzzling inwardly about the tension that had grown between them, and half afraid that she would blow her chances by losing control and telling him exactly what she thought about his behavior, she stood for some moments before her eyes focused on the amount it was for. She almost dropped the check in surprise.

"I can't accept this," she gasped.

"Why not?" he jeered. "Isn't it enough?"

"You must know it's not that," she flung at him, her composure slipping again. "It's too much. I expected you to pay well, but you've gone overboard."

If she presented a check of this amount to Ally, she dared not conjecture what her friend would think she'd had to do to earn it.

For the first time that evening she had said something that neither lowered his brow in displeasure nor lifted his mouth in sarcasm; instead an odd, thoughtful expression stayed for a moment or two on his face.

"Perhaps you're not past redemption, after all," he said. Before she could ask him what he meant by that, he went on to say, "It's not as lavish as it looks at face value. I shall expect you to deduct a portion of that to buy new clothes. Unless your wardrobe is fitted out in readiness for trips of this nature?"

"Of course it isn't. It's hardly an everyday occurrence. Obviously I shall need new clothes." She hadn't thought of that necessity before he drew her attention to it. "But even so, it's still too generous."

"I'm going to be even more generous—" he began.

"Oh, no, you're not," she broke in urgently. "I

haven't yet decided if my conscience will allow me to accept this much."

"Hm. You really are the most extraordinary girl. If you'd let me finish you'd know that I wasn't intending to up the price. My generosity in this instance is not of the monetary sort. I'm going to give you something that money can't buy—time. Time to have second thoughts. I have to leave tomorrow—there's no way I can put off the date of my departure—but I'm going to give you a few days' grace. I'll book you on a flight for, say, early next week. Utilize the time as you think best, winding up your affairs here, shopping for new clothes, or changing your mind. I'll see that your ticket is sent to you by post. Remember, you don't have to use it."

Her throat felt abnormally dry as it occurred to her that he didn't want her to use it. He'd had the second thoughts he said he was hoping she'd have and was looking for a way out. It was all of a piece with what usually happened to her when something wonderful was within her grasp. Something unprecedented always happened to snatch it away.

The prospect of going to the Bahamas and working for this difficult-to-understand man who aroused equal quantities of like and dislike in her, who angered her as much as he appealed to her, was suddenly the most wonderful thing that had ever happend to her in her life.

"And if I don't change my mind?" she queried rebelliously.

"You'll be met at Nassau airport," he said with an unwelcome return of that arrogant, mocking drawl.

Sleep was again a stranger to her that night. Next morning, feeling decidedly under par, looking as she always did when she was tired, heavy-eyed like a drooping child, she could have done without the explicit meaning of Ally's raised left eyebrow, on the heels of which came the verbal comment, "It's not worth it."

"What isn't?"

"Whatever's making you look this jaded."

"I . . . think I'm coming down with a cold," she lied on inspiration. If Ally thought she had any doubts, the check was as good as torn up.

"Oh, poor you. Taken anything for it?"

"No, not yet. Aren't you going to ask me how it went last night?"

"How did it go last night?" Ally asked dutifully, her sober tone showing that she wasn't fooled.

"I got the job," Catherine said. Roused by Ally's suspicion to do better, she matched her brightest tone to her biggest smile. "Didn't I do well? You must have second sight, or something, because you were absolutely right in thinking he'd want me to go with him. Thank goodness it's not a whaler in the Antarctic, but . . ." Pause for dramatic effect before announcing importantly, "The Bahamas, would you believe?"

Ally's mouth fell open in surprise. "Lucky you!"

"Payment in advance."

"No quibble about rates? Some people keep rich by being mean."

"The only quibble was on my side. I said it was too much, but as he so rightly pointed out I shall need to fit myself with a new wardrobe."

She placed the check squarely on the desk in front of Ally. Ally's eyebrows took off into her hair. She didn't offer to touch the check, just stared at it as though it was too hot to handle. "Oh, my! And which fashion house will madam be patronizing?" she said, adopting a high, false accent.

Just in case she wasn't joking and thought the amount on the check might have gone to her head,

Catherine said firmly, "The usual places will do fine for most of the things, with perhaps a couple of special outfits from some not too pricey boutique."

"Can I give you some advice, Cat?"

"Please do. I've always admired your dress sense."

"I don't mean about clothes."

"That sounds as though you're going to tell me something I won't want to know, 'for my own good.'" She pulled at a strand of hair, a subconscious habit in moments of doubt or stress, and released it when she realized what she was doing, but not before Ally's quick eye had spotted the telltale sign.

"My advice is this. Don't consider Allycats. I know it would put us on our feet. While you were away I could find new premises and perhaps move in, and we'd be able to hold on until we've had a chance to make a name for ourselves and the jobs really start rolling in. But weighed against that is how you feel. It's a lot of money. If you're the teeniest bit uneasy about *anything* . . ." Her voice trailed off.

"I'm not," Catherine affirmed. It wasn't exactly a lie. She didn't feel the teeniest bit uneasy. She felt a lot uneasy.

Poor Ally, she could almost sympathize with her, torn as she was between wanting to slam the check straight into the bank and settle back in the knowledge that her most immediate and pressing problem was solved and that as far as the question of Samantha was concerned she could tell her in-laws, "Thank you but no, thank you,"—and guilt because she wasn't using force to talk Catherine out of it.

"It isn't right," Ally said. "Nobody is paid this much for secretarial work. Are they?" She looked at the check again, as though expecting it to acquire a voice and speak up for itself. "It doesn't add up. Just how

many years has he paid you for in advance?" she joked
feebly.

Catherine wondered what her reaction would have
been if she'd told her it was just a retainer. Something
to go on with until he decided if she would suit, in
which case more would follow.

She decided not to risk it and said, "No time period
was specified. Honestly, Ally, it's not what you're
thinking."

"Isn't it?" Ally said, pathetically eager to be convinced.

"Remember Joanna Dunn?"

"Of course. But what's she got to do with it?"

"Nothing. Just drawing a parallel. She's working as a
nanny for a millionaire Greek ship owner. Well, her
salary, after everything's been found for her—keep,
travel, uniforms and so forth—makes our joint earnings
look like pin money."

"Mm, yes." Ally reflected further on that. "I
wouldn't like to say anything to spoil it for you. A
chance like this might never come your way again. The
Bahamas—all expenses paid and more besides. Oh,
Cat, isn't it exciting? If you're sure? When I think about
it properly I'm going to hate you, because nothing like
this has ever happened to me, but right now I'm thrilled
to bits for you. It is all right, isn't it?" She went on in
this way for a while longer, her enthusiasm punctuated
by the odd doubtful murmur, and then asked, giving a
feeling of finality to the situation that took Catherine's
breath away, "When do you go?"

The door of escape had closed so firmly on her that
she thought she should have heard its loud clang.
Gathering herself together, she said, "I won't know for
certain until my plane ticket arrives—it's to be sent
through the post—but he said early next week."

She had such a silly feeling, a mingling of fear and

excitement, as though she sensed that she had just committed herself to something that would change her for life, and she wasn't sure whether she should welcome it or be afraid.

Was it an omen? Paul Hebden's face came brightly to her mind, the distinctive jade eyes dark and disapproving, the strong mouth molded in disdain. She shrugged, trying to dispel the unfriendly image—too late for second thoughts, his or hers. If he hadn't wanted her to take on his typing he shouldn't have asked her in the first place.

Ally gasped, her voice vibrant with wonder, and if she noticed anything wrong with Catherine's expression she didn't comment on it. "I suppose it's all pretty much run of the mill to him; being a celebrity, he's probably used to shooting off somewhere at a moment's notice, but it's not going to give you a lot of time for shopping." She giggled, a lovely, compulsive, infectious sound, pulling Catherine out of her gray mood. "Not that you'll need all that much time now that money's no object. It'll just be a case of going into the most exclusive shop and saying, 'I'll have that, that and that.' I was thinking of the old hunting-for-a-bargain days and all that cheating camouflage stuff you do."

"It's not cheating, it's good strategy," Catherine said, defending her trick of changing cheap belts and buttons for more expensive ones to add a touch of individuality, and buying a longer length than she needed and then cutting off the machine-stitched hem and turning it up again to give it that hand-hemmed haute couture look. "And I am not going on a mad spending spree."

"We'll see about that," Ally declared. "It's time you got something good out of life instead of looking out for others."

Catherine didn't know about that. She did know that

it was pretty wonderful to see Ally looking, talking, acting in the old familiar way when they went shopping together. She'd always gone pelting at life, but of late she'd got into the habit of shrinking into corners, waiting to be pelted at. Yes, whatever happened, it was worth it to see Ally back on top, with an energy and determination and unarguable logic that swept all Catherine's protests to one side.

"Buy this one, Cat. It won't crush in your suitcase. No, no, no, *Catherine!* This one will defy passing fashion whims—how can you say it's expensive when it will last you forever? Oh, you'll make a grand entrance in this." She held up a soft, floating chiffon in subtle shadings of every blue imaginable, including the sapphire blue of Catherine's eyes. "Yes, Cat, I know what you're thinking. But every girl is surely allowed one bit of frivolity, and it's so *you.*"

"You're right. I must be frivolous to let you talk me into it. And why have I bought all this beach wear? This is supposed to be a working assignment. No, not supposed to be, *is.*"

But the holiday feeling persisted.

She decided to give up her small apartment. She felt that it would be too extravagant to keep it and pay rent for even a short period, and anyway, it would give her the impetus to find a better place when she returned. She rented it fully furnished, so she didn't have the problem of putting a lot of bulky furniture into storage. Ally volunteered to give a safe home to her bits and pieces, the pretty trivia she'd picked up to make her place more homelike, until she could take possession again.

There were some things she couldn't bear to part with for even a short time, and these she packed into her suitcase: a handful of treasured photographs; a falling-to-pieces rag doll called Belinda; her mother's very last gift to her, the brush and comb set, complete with its own matching mirror.

She wrapped the mirror carefully and made a nest for it between her clothes. She gave her hair a final brush, resting the ivory back against her cheek for a tender moment before tucking the hairbrush into her suitcase.

Her eyes were bright, but her expression was determined as she closed the lid. Even so, nostalgia bit deep as she silently mouthed: Goodbye old life . . . hello new. . . .

Chapter Four

She had given her suitcase into the care of the airport authorities for it to be loaded onto the plane, said goodbye to Ally and little Samantha, promised to send a card to let them know that she'd arrived safely, and now walked through to the departure lounge to wait for her flight number to be called.

She glanced idly at the other passengers waiting to embark. They were mostly holiday makers, it seemed, families. Here and there she saw a more soberly dressed lone traveler wearing that distinctive air of business as if it were an extra garment. And there was one eye-catching female, also on her own, who looked as though she could have done with an extra garment— a jacket, for instance, to cover a skimpy top that would have looked better on a beach than in the busy lounge of an international airport. The top was outrageously if fittingly teamed with the tightest pair of trousers imaginable.

Catherine's eyes lingered a moment longer, almost in horrified fascination, not quite dismissing the woman as a brash blonde, guessing instinctively that the girl would have a nature as generous as her body, which would have been superb in the right clothes. Strangely, because Ally was stick-slender and would only have come up to the other woman's shoulders and they didn't share one similar feature, she reminded Catherine of Ally. Both gave out the same waves of electric animation—nothing done in moderation, no half measures. That was how Ally had been before Ray's death left her lost and disoriented, and how she had been the last few days, showing such unselfish delight in helping Catherine to get organized for this trip.

For once there was no frustrating delay and they boarded the plane on time. Predictable. Paul Hebden would be there to meet her at the other end, and anything he had a finger in wouldn't dare to be subjected to life's petty irritations.

She was shown to a window seat. Lovely! Had he arranged that, too?

A sound at her side made her look up to see who her companion for the flight was going to be, and she saw with a mixture of amusement and dismay that it was the woman in the skimpy top and tight trousers. Paul Hebden certainly hadn't arranged this. She would not meet with his approval at all!

She had a clutter of possessions with her which she divided between the overhead baggage compartment and the floor, before turning her vivacious smile on Catherine.

"Hi! I'm Deirdre Patterson. What's your handle?"

"Catherine Mason."

At first Catherine was reluctant to be drawn into conversation, but gradually Deirdre's brash, extroverted charm began to take effect. Simply by looking into her face, Catherine knew that wherever she went, fun and laughter wouldn't be far behind.

"I'm staying at the Ocean Beach Hotel," Deirdre said chattily. "Which hotel are you booked at?"

"I don't know," she replied truthfully.

She wasn't normally forthcoming about her private affairs to strangers, but something in Deirdre's expres-

sion told her that this had come out sounding too
abrupt, as if she were deliberately withholding the
name of her hotel in case the blond woman had
thoughts of getting in touch with her once they were
settled in.

Not wanting to sound unkind, she said, "I really
don't know. I'm not on holiday. I'm going out to work.
My employer will have made the arrangements and I'm
expecting to be met at the airport."

Deirdre's eyebrows lifted in surprise. "I had you
figured out as a rich society girl, hopping from one
luscious holiday spot to another. Your clothes fooled
me. I know—with your fantastic figure it's obvious.
You're in the glamour and beauty business. You're the
editor of a glossy magazine. Or—better still—a top
photographic model and you can afford to dress like
that because you get a discount. Anywhere near the
mark?"

"Not even vaguely close. I'm a down-to-earth shorthand typist and until now I've led a very mundane life.
If someone had told me a week ago that I—" There was
something about this woman that encouraged confi-
dences. Halting her runaway tongue, she said, "What
about you, Deirdre? What sort of work do you do that
pays well enough for you to take exotic holidays?"

"I'm a hair stylist and—no, the tips aren't that
good." The animation slid from her face, her buoyancy
snapping as suddenly as if it had been severed with a
knife. "I'm twenty-five years old. Since I was sixteen
I've been going with this guy, and for the past three
years or more I've been saving like mad to chip in with
the mortgage. Then, out of the blue, he packed me in. I
dried my tears and took a long hard look at him, and I
said to myself, 'Deirdre, love, you must be nuts. What
can he give you except a houseful of kids and years of
scrimping and saving and making do?' Surely I was

born for better things than that? I asked myself why I should waste myself on someone who couldn't give me the things I so richly deserved and told myself that it was about time I found someone who could. Snag was, there aren't that many millionaires going begging where I live. So I had all this mortgage money in the bank and no other use for it, so I thought, why don't I go where they are? I've been kicked, now it's my turn. From now on I'm out for all I can get. I've got three weeks to find myself a rich husband, and I'm not too fussy whose husband he is. I suppose a nice refined girl like you is shocked by that," she concluded with a touch of defiance.

"Not so much shocked as concerned. Man-hunting has become a fashionable holiday pastime, but like a lot of other sports, it can be dangerous. I don't think you're as tough as you make out, and I think you could get hurt even worse than before."

"Sure I could. That's the luck of the draw. I could just as easily fall into a life of luxury."

"I hope you do, Deirdre," Catherine said, and meant it.

The murmur of voices around them increased, growing excited as the first of the islands that formed the Bahama group came into view, denoting that the long journey was nearing its end. Soon other islands appeared; Catherine strained to look down at the scattered specks on the ocean which grew larger as the wings of the jetliner swept lower.

The pilot identified the islands by name over the communication system, giving tantalizing snippets of information about them that whetted her appetite to know more, especially about the privately owned cays. She saw the blue-green sea edged with creamy-white surf and beaches bleached white by centuries of sunshine. It was an unspoiled, unsurpassed beauty because of its centuries of neglect since Columbus dismissed the islands as mere stopping places. The "useless islands," King Ferdinand was reputed to have called them. He had certainly been proved wrong.

She realized with a new upsurge of excitement that they were now above New Providence and its satellite Paradise Island, connected by the spectacular Potter's Cay Bridge. Towering hotel blocks and moving cars alike were reduced to toy proportions. The plane banked and she had a dizzy kaleidoscopic impression of sparkling blue water, yachts and cruise ships—which was hastily cut off, along with her circulation, by the urgent grip of Deirdre's fingers 'round her wrist.

The blond girl moaned, "My stomach! I wish I hadn't gone mad with the duty free."

Catherine had thought that Deirdre was drinking too much, but she hadn't liked to stress the point beyond cautioning that she'd read somewhere that alcohol was more potent while you were airborne. She felt that once you started moralizing with someone like Deirdre, it would be difficult to know when to stop.

"You'll be all right. We're landing now," she said, offering sympathy.

Hardly had she got the words out than the wheels hit the ground and, with an increased rush of noise, the jet taxied along the landing strip.

Her window seat immediately lost its appeal. She was trapped where she was until Deirdre decided to move, and Deirdre, looking very wan indeed, seemed incapable of doing so.

"Deirdre?"

"I feel dreadful."

"I promise that you'll feel better once you're outside. Come on, I'll help you with your hand luggage."

"Thanks. You're a pal," Deirdre said faintly.

Wondering how anyone could pack so haphazardly, Catherine shared the untidy assortment, taking Deirdre's rucksack and her bulging plastic carrier bag as well as her own neat shoulder travel-bag, leaving Deirdre to cope with her own canvas bag and camera. They seemed to be all she was capable of carrying.

As they waited for the main luggage to be unloaded, Deirdre blossomed into life. "Sorry about that. I'm fine now, though, just as you said I would be. Look—your boss is sure to give you some time off, so how about getting in touch with me at my hotel and we can go out on the town together, mm?"

Catherine didn't dislike Deirdre; in fact, there was something rather likable and quite touching about the girl. But it would be miserable to go out on the town with her. She was delighted to be able to render a friendly brushoff.

"I'd love that, but I doubt if it will be possible. The island isn't all that big, I know, but transport could be a problem. I mean, it's unlikely that we'll find ourselves on the same part of the island. I don't even know if I'll be staying in New Providence. For all I know Nasseau airport might be just a convenient place for my employer to meet me before going to one of the out islands."

"Oh, well, I can hope that you get in touch," Deirdre responded cheerfully, before adding on an ominous note, "I shall be glad when I get my suitcase. I have a friend whose suitcase went missing en route and it spoiled her holiday."

A foreboding chill shivered through Catherine's system as she thought what it would mean to her if she lost her suitcase.

"Don't look so glum," Deirdre said. "We can't both lose our suitcases, so if yours goes missing I'll lend you something to wear. My suitcase is full to bursting with pretties."

Catherine hadn't been thinking of all her newly purchased, beautiful clothes, but of the irreplaceable things . . . the loss of her hairbrush set, her mother's last gift to her, would be tragic.

Despite her fears, she had to smile at Deirdre's words. Everything about Deirdre was "full to bursting." Her poorly-matched assortment of hand luggage, her magnificent bosom in her skimpy top.

Their suitcases were retrieved without mishap and Catherine released a long, thankful sigh. The rest of the airport formalities were soon cleared.

Deirdre was still clinging to her like a limpet. If the woman couldn't manage her hand luggage she certainly couldn't manage a heavy suitcase as well, so there was no possibility of casting her adrift until a porter had been found. This, apparently, was not going to be easy. Catherine wondered what it was about herself that landed her in situations of this nature. She always seemed to get lumbered with likable people, first Ally, and now Deirdre, who were incapable of managing their own affairs.

"You say you're being met?" Deirdre asked with cunning speculation.

"Yes." She got the drift of Deirdre's thoughts— obviously she was hoping for a lift. She didn't have to put on a helpless expression and say, "I hope taxis are easier to come by than porters."

Catherine hoped so, too. Failing that, she hoped that Paul wouldn't be there to meet her himself, but that he would have sent someone else to collect her. It took no imagination at all to guess that Paul's attitude to Deirdre would be one of disdain. Strangely enough, Catherine found that she didn't care that it might annoy Paul to be taken out of his way to give Deirdre a lift, but that she felt sorry for Deirdre herself. She knew what it was like to flinch under the power of Paul's

disapproval, although she hadn't yet worked out what
he disapproved of in her, and she didn't want Deirdre
to be hurt or embarrassed. Oh, Lord, she thought, it's
an Ally deal again. Because she felt protective toward
Deirdre, even though she could give Catherine three
years.

Deirdre let out an appreciative gasp. "Wow! Get a
load of him."

Catherine knew even before she turned her head that
she would see a man who was eminently worthy of
Deirdre's admiration and had a long-suffering expression on his face, as if he were bored by it.

Yes, there he was, tall, suntanned and lean, a
commanding blond god of a man who would always
find himself under the surveillance of feminine eyes
wherever he went. It was amusing to note that the eyes
of every woman in the place were on him, and a flicker
of sympathy went through her because she felt that in
his shoes she too would have found it too much of a
good thing, and that very probably she would have
responded in much the same way as he did.

The bored weariness in his jade green eyes hadn't
escaped Deirdre's notice. "Good looking—and doesn't
he know it, the arrogant devil!" But her voice quickly
changed its tone as he began to walk toward them.
"Ooops! He's coming over. Which one of us do you
suppose he intends to pick up?"

"Me," Catherine said stoically. "He's Paul Hebden,
my employer."

"R–e–a–l–l–y!" Deirdre drawled out. The meal she
made of that simple word, and the meaning she put into
it, were nothing to the meal she was making of him with
her eyes.

Paul's attention was fixed not on Deirdre, but on
Catherine. Not on her good cream suit which was
already shedding the creases it had collected on the

plane, not on the stark simplicity and bandbox freshness of her pure silk blouse, not even on the pleading appeal to be nice on her face, which did not match up to her clothes and was showing signs of fatigue—but on the messy conglomeration of luggage in her hands. He thought they belonged to her!

At that precise moment the plastic carrier bag decided that it had had enough and a split developed in its side which in turn released an aerosol can of hairspray which rolled toward Paul's feet.

He bent, picked it up, walked the few remaining steps, froze her with a withering look and said, "Yours, I believe."

"It's Deirdre's, actually," she said haughtily, feeling mean at drawing attention to the fact that Deirdre was the sloppy packer, but overjoyed to see the supercilious smirk very nearly turn into a smile.

He made no audible comment and she had to take that as an acknowledgment of her victory.

She performed the introductions and his manner toward Deirdre was on the very edge of civility, but at least it didn't drop into rudeness, which was something to be thankful for.

"I'm staying at the Ocean Beach Hotel," Deirdre volunteered. "That wouldn't by any chance be on your way?"

"It would. May I give you a lift?"

"How very kind of you to suggest it. Thank you, that would be most convenient," Deirdre said, moistening her full mouth and pouting seductively at him.

Catherine looked on in growing despair. No wonder he held her sex in contempt when the majority of them behaved toward him as Deirdre was doing, flaunting her voluptuous body at him, sending him a message through veiled eyes that few red-blooded men could mistake for anything but what it was.

She was conscious that Paul had transferred his glance back to her and she tried to erase the stony disapproval on her mouth. He might, just might, think she was feeling possessive toward him, even jealous of Deirdre's easy ability to flirt with him, and nothing could be further from the truth. The color in her cheeks was embarrassment that Deirdre could cheapen herself in such a way; the red there had certainly not been roused by the green-eyed monster.

Whatever interpretation Paul had arrived at was not revealed by his expression or his next words. "I have a car parked quite near by. All the same, I think we need . . ." Without elaborating on that, his cool glance lifted from Catherine to scan the possibilities, the quick imperious jerk of his head all that was needed to summon up a porter out of thin air.

Catherine joined the lordly procession to the car, fuming inwardly and perilously close to—oh, help, no!—not tears! Self-pity would be the last straw. Yet would it have hurt him to show some sign that she was welcome? She found herself gnawing again on the puzzle. Why had he asked her to come if he didn't want her there? On the plane, in the odd moments when her mind had struggled free of Deirdre's incessant chatter, she had asked herself that question. In the end she had gone half way to convincing herself that she had imagined his unfriendly attitude. Apparently she hadn't. If anything, his manner had grown even icier.

They stopped at Deirdre's hotel to drop her off. Paul got out of the car with her to summon a porter to carry her baggage.

"Now don't you forget," Deirdre said on bidding them goodbye. "If it's at all possible, get in touch with me and we can go out somewhere and have fun."

"Will do," Catherine agreed feebly, wishing Deirdre

hadn't repeated her invitation in Paul's hearing. "Goodbye. Have a good time."

"I intend to," Deirdre said, winking cheekily. "'Bye."

Once they were on their way again Catherine said, keeping her eyes fixed front, not wishing to look at Paul's forbidding profile, "Thank you for giving Deirdre a lift."

"It was on our route," he replied ungraciously. "I hope you didn't mean it when you said you'd contact her."

Of course she hadn't meant it. "Would you have preferred me to tell her the blunt truth, that we have nothing in common and that her idea of fun certainly isn't mine?" she tossed at him impatiently.

"No." His laugh was harsh. "You're not a fun girl, are you? It's strictly business with you."

Obviously he was digging at her because she'd turned down his invitation to have dinner with him back in England.

"There's a time for fun and a time for business. I don't believe in combining the two," she said firmly.

"We've arrived," he said brusquely, slamming the brakes on so fiercely that if she hadn't been wearing a seatbelt she would have shot straight through the windshield.

He didn't offer to get out of the car, just turned to look at her. "Don't get in touch with your brash blond friend," he said savagely.

"Is that an order?"

"Yes."

She was too incensed to speak. She hadn't intended to seek Deirdre out, she didn't particularly fancy an outing with her, but she would not knuckle under. Paul couldn't keep her working every minute of the day. He would have to allow her some free time in which to do whatever she wished. If she was within striking distance of Deirdre she might just change her mind and take her up on her invitation.

She opened her mouth to say as much, but closed it again without uttering a word. She had risen early, it had been a long, tiring journey and she was wilting under the delicious, incredible heat.

"Well?" he demanded, reading her silence and detecting mutiny.

"I'm too weary to disagree with you," she replied with a certain brave dignity.

On both sides it was a most unsatisfactory way to end an argument, but at least it had the effect of dinting his composure. She didn't at all mind making him feel guilty, she felt that his behavior rated it, but she could have done without the minute inspection of her face, which was minus makeup and looking decidedly worse for wear.

He took her hand away from the strand of hair she was unconsciously fiddling with and said stiffly, "I'm sorry." Apparently apologizing didn't come easy to him. "It's inconsiderate of me to harass you or to detain you for a moment longer than is necessary from the cool shower you're obviously longing to take."

He got out of the car, snapped his fingers and a man came running toward him to receive the keys of the rented car.

"Garage it, Joseph, and bring Miss Mason's baggage up."

The man, a Bahamian, gave him a teeth-flashing smile and would have moved 'round to Catherine's side of the car to assist her out, had not Paul waved him away, intent on doing that job himself.

"Come," he said, opening the door for her and

taking her elbow to guide her first into the hotel and then into the lift which transported them to their floor.

"We have adjacent rooms," he said, stopping at a door and opening it for her. "Your luggage shouldn't be long. I'll come back when you've taken your shower."

The pat he gave her bottom to send her inside was excessively familiar, but not distasteful.

She thought that she would wait for her luggage to arrive before she took her shower. In any case she wanted to look at and gloat over her room. It was more luxurious than any hotel room she had ever been in before. The bathroom was tiled in palest green. She resisted its cool invitation to inspect the elegant simplicity of the furniture, which provided masses of drawer and hanging space; the wide double bed, instead of the single she had expected; the welcoming touch of a vase of bright, exotic flowers.

She wandered out onto the balcony and the view that met her eyes took her breath away. Casuarinas wafted gently in a breeze that was as soft as silk against her cheek. White sand. Translucent sea reflecting many textures of color, taking its mood from the changing tones of the sky.

With the feel of Paul's hand still tingling through her body she asked herself how she was going to hold herself aloof from him in these unreal surroundings. It wasn't just like being in a different part of the world; it was like being in another world altogether. Unreal sky, unreal noises, unreal smells. The air was laden with the distinctive, heavy scent of some unidentified blossom. Carried to her on the breeze, it was drugging, hypnotic almost, drawing her into the unreality so that she was no longer sensible, circumspect, even slightly prim Catherine Mason, who could have repulsed Paul's hand just now, but a strange wild creature who frightened herself with her own wayward thoughts and who was on the brink of running headlong into self-destruction.

She sighed so deeply that it was almost a groan. She could have stayed out on the balcony for much longer, just looking, soaking up all the beauty before her, but she knew that time was getting on. The light was changing even as she watched; the brilliant glare that had been an assault to her unaccustomed eyes was leaving the sun, and the sky was a kinder, less vivid blue. The view would be there for her tomorrow. For tonight there was a shower to be taken, dinner to be looked forward to, and one more door in her bedroom still to be investigated.

Did it communicate with Paul's bedroom? She tried the knob less gingerly than she would have done had she not been absolutely certain in her mind that it would be locked. She gasped in astonishment when it yielded under her fingers and she found herself looking into a connecting sitting room between the two bedrooms. She knew this because the door on the opposite wall was ajar and to her consternation she was not only looking straight into Paul's bedroom, but straight at Paul himself.

He turned his head, answering her startled gaze with one of inquiry. "Are you all right?"

"Yes, thank you," she said, hastily closing the door on his mocking jade eyes.

She supposed the reason there was no key in the lock was because it gave entry into a shared sitting room. It meant, and this was the disconcerting part, that Paul could just walk in on her any time he was so minded. She could ask for a key, but if she did, would it look as though she was making an issue out of it, even serve to put ideas into his head?

The Bahamian porter arrived with her luggage. She decided not to unpack properly. Her clothes wouldn't come to any harm for having to spend a few more hours in her suitcase. So she carefully took out the things she needed right away. Toiletries and makeup, her precious hairbrush set, a bathrobe, and a dress and evening sandals to go down to the dining room. On a last minute impulse she'd packed the book she'd recently bought, the one written by Paul, and as this was right at the top she took it out and put it on the bedside table. She remembered to fish out her shower cap. She would have liked to stand directly under the jet of water, but she was really hungry and didn't want to have to wait for her hair to dry before eating.

Emerging from the bathroom, feeling tingly and clean, she was taken aback to see Paul in her room.

"You certainly took your time," he said. "I was on the point of coming in to get you."

"What are you doing in my room?" she demanded coolly.

"I said I'd come back for you when you'd had your shower. Well, I have." Doubtless he saw the way her eyes turned to the keyless communicating door, because then he said, "We also share the same balcony. I came in that way. Cozy, isn't it?"

She was glad she had taken the precaution of putting on her bathrobe before coming out of the bathroom. All the same, she wished there were a little more of it. The neckline was all right, but she would have preferred it to be longer and was conscious of the amount of leg it exposed.

She expected him to make some comment about her legs, he'd certainly had a good enough look at them, but his eyes flicked over to the book on the bedside table, his book, and it prompted him to say, "You've got a hot taste in bedtime reading."

"You should know," she said, more than a little puzzled by his comment.

In case he thought she was a fan of his it would have been honest to admit that it was the only book of his she'd ever bought, but her slight hesitation lost her the opportunity to speak up.

"Have you ever been to the tropics before?" he asked abruptly.

"No."

"That's what I thought. That's why I wanted to hurry you out of the bathroom. Dawn is the best time to be up and about on a tropical island, but the sunset is the most spectacular sight you'll ever see. Your first tropical sunset is an experience you'll never forget. I quite envy you. I'm glad I'm here to share the moment with you."

He held out his hand to her and her own went into it without hesitation. He led her out to the balcony, putting her in front of his lean frame, resting his hands lightly, not in a distracting way, on her shoulders.

He was right. It was magnificent. Dramatic and beautiful. And the colors—pinks and blues and mauves. So incredible. It began with bits of bluish pink turning into blood-red splashes which quickly changed to mauve. Mauve and purple swathes draped the clouds and slid across the horizon. When it was over, and it was quite dark, the afterglow remained in her heart. She stood, absolutely motionless, savoring it in silent homage.

The hands on her shoulders tightened their grip, turning her fully 'round into his arms. She was conscious of his fingers dealing with the tightly secured knot on the sash of her bathrobe, the sensation of air circulating 'round her body as the robe loosened from her waist. Her heart was palpitating wildly. She had never been so close to a man, so scantily clothed— because beneath the bathrobe there was only her—in the whole of her life. It wasn't right. But on this night that was surely made for lovers, how could it *not* be right?

His hand touched her trembling mouth before sliding along her shoulder and across her back.

She must speak up or it would be too late. Somehow, summoning up a superhuman effort, she found her voice, hoping its aching reluctance didn't betray her true desire. "I'm hungry, Paul."

"So am I, but not for food."

"I couldn't eat on the plane."

"Later—we'll eat later."

"Later I'll be asleep," she said, using her weariness to prevent something happening which she wanted desperately at this moment, but which she knew she would regret when she was her normal self again.

She had said the right thing. It secured her immediate release.

"I'm being inconsiderate again. Run along and get dressed and then we'll go down to the dining room. I'll wait for you in the sitting room."

But once he'd gone, and she was back in her room again, she didn't fly into action. She stood awhile, clutching her bathrobe more closely 'round her, waiting for the trembling in her limbs to subside and the ache of longing to diminish.

The intimacies, the pat on her bottom and the audacious way he had unfastened her bathrobe and slid his hands underneath, had been far from distasteful to her, had given her pleasure. Oh, dear Lord, what was happening to her?

She couldn't even draw comfort from the thought that he'd tricked her, because she had seen through him. Back in England she had known that his coldness was a deliberate ploy to get her there, which he would then drop. But the puzzle was becoming more tangled and mystifying, because the coldness hadn't dropped.

The ice was still there; something was seriously disturbing him, but whatever it was it was unable to quash his hunger for her. If it had just been a case of working out his normal male passions on a woman he would have had plenty of takers. Deirdre had all but served herself up on a plate for him, and made it patently obvious that she would be happy to oblige any time he crooked his finger. But he hadn't wanted Deirdre. He wanted *her*, perhaps for no better reason than that she had resisted his earlier advances, and he intended to pursue her until he got her. You might as well face up to it, she told herself. You've thrown your lot in with a calculating and tenacious charmer who won't give up until he gets you into bed.

She might have been able to cope with that. A situation faced up to was half way to being solved; at least, she'd always thought so. What she couldn't seem to cope with was herself. Her worry about his motivations was nowhere near as great as her worry over her own inability to deal with the reaction of this person who inhabited her body, this woman who looked like her, spoke with her voice and bore her name, but who harbored thoughts and desires which, less than a week ago, would have shocked her to the core of her being.

His passions she could handle; it was her own that were causing her concern. She could hardly believe such a wanton, shameful, humiliating thing of herself, but she had wanted him as much as he had wanted her.

Chapter Five

She woke next morning to the sound of birds, though it was different somehow from the usual birdsong her ears were accustomed to; and to the uncanny feeling that someone was looking down at her.

As she lifted her eyelids and saw that it was Paul who stood by her bed, her cheeks turned rosy not so much from sleep as from the memory of what had passed between them the night before on the balcony—and afterward.

The balcony incident had tied her emotions in knots. Coupled with her fatiguing day of travel, it had resulted in her loss of appetite. When Paul had eventually escorted her down to the hotel dining room she had been too tired to do more than push her food around on her plate. When he had solicitously suggested that they "turn in" she'd nodded eagerly, grateful to be released. The dining room was too bright and crowded. The clatter of cutlery and the garrulous mingling of voices were beginning to have a jarring effect on her already strung-up nerves, and she was finding it increasingly difficult to keep a social smile on her lips. The thought of her bed in the dark solitude of her quiet room had been infinitely appealing. It had come as a shock, if not a total surprise, when Paul had hesitated by her door, seemingly reluctant to continue to his own room.

"Good-night, Paul," she had instructed coolly. Because that was what it had been, an instruction to move on and a firm put down to the inquiry in his eyes.

Had he really expected to be invited in? The dark frown hardening his features had answered that unspoken thought and increased her misgivings. Yes, no doubt about it, he had expected to come into her room, with everything that implied.

Her indignation of the night before renewed itself with vigor at this current intrusion on her privacy. She was annoyed to think that he'd been watching her while she slept and it blasted into her voice at full volume. "Do you mind!"

"Mind what?" He had the audacity to look taken aback.

"Going. What else? In future, it would be polite to knock—and wait for permission before you enter."

"It's like that, is it?"

"Like what?"

"Last night, jet lag. Yes, that was in order. What's it this morning? The big rip off? No way will I go along with that."

"I think you should explain that remark."

"You do? That's a laugh." But there was no mirth or humor on his face.

She recoiled as his contempt brought a fresh reminder of that scene before dinner when he had untied her bathrobe with such familiarity. His fingers should never have been allowed to slide underneath, she realized with a rush of shame which deepened the color in her cheeks. Instead of trembling like an excited, overheated schoolgirl and making excuses about being hungry, she ought to have rebuffed him instantly and with no trace of indecision, to let him know where he stood. Had he taken it into his head that, by not doing so, she had been stringing him along? Playing hard to get as a

face-saving gesture, because it wasn't seemly to appear
too eager?

"I should think you would feel ashamed!" he
sneered, mistaking consternation for guilt as she avert-
ed her gaze. "Little Alley Cat. The name you and your
conniving partner call yourselves is spot on. Do you
take it in turns, or does she always send you because of
your air of purity and your big innocent eyes?"

She gasped in indignation at the insult. If she was at a
loss for words, he still had a mouthful to churn out.

"You can take it from me, they're not going to stay
innocent, not this time. When I've finished with you
you'll have lost that kitten-faced butter-wouldn't-melt
look. The butter will fry."

"This is absurd," she finally managed in near desperation.

"Drop the pretense and accept that this time you've
met your match." The anger gathering within him
showed in the muscle working in his cheek, communicating itself to her so that she crossed her hands in front
of herself and cringed away from him as though in fear
of what was coming next.

If she hadn't done so she didn't think he would have
offered to touch her, but the unconscious action incited
him. He dragged her hands away and pulled down the
elasticized neck of her cotton nightgown, exposing the
firm creamy flesh of her full breasts, and surely also
the tumultuous beating of her heart.

"No, Paul!" she cried out.

"No?" he mocked.

"Don't you know what no means?" she screamed at
him.

"I guess not."

"It probably isn't a word you hear very often."

"You're beneath contempt," he spat at her. "I

thought it was only morals you lacked, and that was bad enough. Now I see that you're without principles, as well. Even in your game there's a code of conduct to be observed. All right, it's 'no' again, but only for the moment. I came to tell you that I've ordered breakfast and it should be up in approximately five minutes. We'll take it on the balcony, and consider yourself lucky that I've a bigger appetite for food than I have for you."

"I don't think I could eat anything."

"That's up to you. You'll put on a wrap or something and come out and watch me eat if you don't want anything yourself."

He turned and left the room with an abruptness that broke her calm like a plate shattering on a stone floor. She dragged her nightgown back into place and lay back on her pillow, her composure in pieces. She couldn't understand what it was about. She thought he'd got angry at her when she turned away from him, rather than at something she'd said. What had he expected her to do? Invite him into her bed? Did he think that because he'd engaged her to do his typing he had an automatic right to have sex with her? But then he'd accused her of being without morals and principles. And what could he have meant by "even in your game"? Their conversations never went anywhere. They always seemed to be talking at cross-purposes. Nothing made sense. She couldn't understand any of it.

It was raining. It had rained for days. Ally sat at her desk, the keys of her typewriter idle as she stared out at the blighted English sky and the dripping spectacle of polished rooftops and pavements, the swift moving convoy of umbrellas and heads bowed under turned-up collars, and thought about Catherine soaking up the Bahamian sunshine. She was nice enough to hope that

Catherine was having a super time, and human enough to feel a little envious that she wasn't sharing it with her.

The door of Allycats opened and she dragged her thoughts from luxury living, coral sands and a fantasy flight of flamingos over a blue lagoon, and looked up to see a man. He was quite tall and pale complexioned, not unattractive in a homely sort of way, with kindly eyes behind brown-rimmed spectacles.

"Good morning," she said brightly, not unhappy to be diverted from her thoughts. "Can I help you?"

"Are you Miss Mason—Catherine Mason?"

"No, I'm Alison Butler, Ally, Catherine's partner in Allycats. Catherine's lapping it up in the Bahamas at the moment."

"On a day like this I'm inclined to say, lucky girl. I didn't particularly want to see Miss Mason. I'm sure you can look after me just as well. I asked for your partner because her name was given to me by a mutual acquaintance who said I might be able to talk you into doing some typing for me."

"Please keep talking. We've only recently started up in business and, well—this might not be in my own best interest, but at least it's honest—we need all the work we can get, Mr. . . . ?"

"Chance. Lucian Chance."

Ally's mouth fell open in dismay. "Not Lucky Chance? The author?"

"For my sins, yes."

"B–but . . . it's not possible . . . oh *no!*" she gasped out, putting her hands to her face.

"It's all right. You don't have to say another word. I understand perfectly."

"You do?" Ally said, gulping hugely.

"It's not an unusual situation, not to me. It happens all the time."

"It does?"

"Yes. So don't look so horror-struck. I can't keep a decent secretary. I have a terrible job getting my manuscripts typed. People say they will before they've read my work, then dash out to buy one of my books to be able to say they've read me—and then immediately back out of the deal. It's obviously the other way 'round with you. Apparently you have read my books and so you're saying no to begin with. I can understand that. Someone like you would find it too embarrassing to type the sort of stuff I write."

"You've got it all wrong, Mr. Chance. You don't understand at all. I wouldn't find it one little bit embarrassing. I'm a fan of yours. I've read every book you've written and I'm waiting avidly for the next. I'll admit that I get my eyebrows singed from time to time while reading some of the more intimate love scenes, but typing them wouldn't bother me. I've enough common sense to know that if you toned down the sex and left all the other hard-punching stuff in, you'd upset the balance. And it's never for sensationalism, but always essential to the plot. And in any case," she said, smiling shyly, "I bet it's the parts that singe the eyebrows that get a second reading."

"You could just be right, Miss Butler."

She'd correct him later and tell him it was Mrs. Butler and explain that she was a widow. Now she said, "Call me Ally, it's friendlier."

"I'd prefer Alison, if I may? But only on the understanding that you call me Lucian. If you're not squeamish about tackling my work and not likely to fall into a purple faint over your typewriter, would you mind telling me just what it is that's upsetting you?"

"We thought, Catherine and I, that Lucky Chance was a purely fictitious name. There's been a mix-up somewhere along the line. Let's try to figure it out.

Starting with—I know! I believe you attended the same party. Well, Lois, your hostess, pointed a man out to Catherine—Lucky Chance, the writer—and mentioned that he might be interested in sending some work our way. Catherine must have latched on to the wrong man." Her brow crinkled and she said without much hope, "There couldn't have been two writers at the party, I suppose?"

"I didn't meet the other one, if there were, so it's doubtful."

Ally nodded soberly. "I'm compelled to agree. It would have been a common bond and Lois would have been bound to introduce you if there had been a fellow writer there. So—if he didn't engage Catherine to type his manuscript, what did he engage her to do?"

Catherine knew that it was no good skulking in bed. Paul had said breakfast in five minutes and if she didn't present herself on the balcony he was capable of fetching her. Better to go voluntarily than be dragged there by force.

Five minutes gave her time to brush her teeth and splash water on her face, but barely allowed her to sort out something to wear. The intimacy of having breakfast with him while still wearing her nightgown, even with the addition of her robe, was not to be contemplated.

She opened her suitcase and carefully extracted a white sundress and, without wasting time on digging out a strapless bra, slid it hurriedly over her head. The skirt was full, with patch pockets set at a jaunty angle. The top gently skimmed her breasts and was dependent on a single length of cotton rope, looped through a ring at the front of the bodice and then tied at the nape of her neck, to stay up. She slid her feet into the canvas mules she'd taken out of her suitcase the night before that doubled as slippers. Half a dozen strokes with her hairbrush and she was as ready as she would ever be. Drawing a deep breath for courage she walked out onto the balcony just as the waiter finished setting the breakfast table and turned to leave.

Her eyes paid compliment to the table setting, the delicate breakfast service and the attractively laid out food: toast, rolls, preserves and fruit, slices of pineapple and papaya. And fruit juice.

She looked up to find that Paul was contemplating her, but his jade green eyes unnervingly registered neither approval nor disapproval, merely viewed her with cold dispassion. She got the feeling that there was still a lot of boiling going on behind that controlled exterior and thought it might be best not to say anything that could trigger his anger again. Of course, that was a somewhat difficult decision when she didn't know what she'd done to make him angry with her in the first place.

"Sit." His terse command made her jump—startling her out of her thoughts—and was easy to obey. "Now eat some breakfast."

That also wasn't going to be as hard to obey as she would have imagined, not when everything looked so tempting.

She reached for the coffee pot. "Shall I pour yours?" she asked tentatively.

"You might as well do something toward earning that fat check I gave you," he replied. "Black, no sugar."

To match your mood, she thought, but let herself be guided by the grim look on his face and forced herself to keep up the pretense of seeing nothing amiss. Although how long she could take his strange behavior without losing control and letting fly with her own temper she dared not think. For the time being, until she could work out what this was all about, she thought this was the best way.

She took a sip of her coffee and found that it tasted as good as its tempting aroma had promised it would. She bypassed the rolls, even though their straight-from-the-oven smell was equally tempting, and decided to try the papaya, which she had never tasted before. In appearance it was not all that unlike melon, except that it was a deeper color, a rich orange. A wedge of lemon sat in its scooped out center. Was it for decoration, or was it to . . . ?

"Squeeze the lemon over the fruit," Paul said, correctly reading her thoughts.

After following his instruction she dug out a spoonful of the fruit. The lemon gave it a lovely tangy flavor. Without this addition it would have been too sweet for her taste, but with it, it was delicious.

When she put her spoon down and sat back in her chair, he said, "Is that all you're going to have?" Then he reached for another roll.

Was he being solicitous? Or was he sneering at her because he knew that under the scrutiny of his steely gaze she found it difficult to eat?

"I've had plenty, thank you," she said.

"For what? Are you trying to go into a decline or something? You couldn't eat dinner last night. You said you'd eaten practically nothing on the plane. And what you've eaten just now wouldn't keep a sparrow alive."

Her chin lifted. "Hasn't it occurred to you that my loss of appetite last night and this morning could be your fault?"

"My fault?"

"It's unnerving, the way you look at me. I wish you'd stop it."

"Stop *looking* at you? First I mustn't touch, now I

mustn't look." No doubt about it, he was definitely ridiculing her. "Most girls would consider it an insult if they'd gone to special lengths to look attractive and a man didn't look."

His emotions were still clamped under ice. It wasn't natural. His anger was too tightly controlled and she was afraid of the consequences if it should suddenly snap. Even in her anxiety the implication that she looked attractive to him pleased her, though. But had she gone to special lengths? Surely this white sundress, which, admittedly, she'd bought initially because she thought it would find favor in his eyes, had been the first thing that came to hand? No, that wasn't true. She felt sickened inside because things had reached a sorry state when she tried to lie to herself. The sundress had been in the middle of her suitcase and she'd had to delve for it.

"You're being deliberately obtuse," she accused. "You know what I mean."

"Do I? That's a debatable point." He rose from his chair and came 'round to her side of the table, then sat on the corner of it, his legs stretched out in front of him. It would have been an innocent posture but for the fact that her chair was next to the balcony rail so that, in effect, he was trapping her.

The feeling of menace was intensified by the cynical way his mouth twisted as he said, "Do you deny dressing to please me?"

"I most certainly do," she said, feeling that his arrogance justified the lie.

His leg moved a fraction closer to press against hers, yet the strongest feeling of restriction was in her throat as she battled with her thoughts. She was suddenly and overwhelmingly aware of the frailty of her own body, which he could crush in his strong hands. She trembled at this never-before-experienced sensation of feeling fragile, of being helplessly at the mercy of his strength and virility. His broad shoulders cut off the sun, but her eyes were still dazzled, not by the strong rays, but by the brilliance and incandescence of him, by the impressive force of his personality, which governed her heartbeat, held her breath and possessed her thoughts to the exclusion of all else. The sun warmed her body and gave her life; he had only just entered her life, and yet he had the power to give it a whole new meaning. That was the startling and disquieting realization that stunned her.

A low laugh rumbled from his throat. "Whether you dressed to please me or not is immaterial, because you do. Very much. Pretty," he said, touching the cotton rope that held up her bodice, the laughter increasing as his fingers followed the rope 'round to her nape.

It needed but the slightest tug to disrobe her, and they were both aware of it.

He was teasing her; surely he wouldn't do it. Not out there on the balcony in full daylight. A very private balcony to be sure, but it was still possible that someone might see.

She dared not take the risk. "Please don't, Paul. Please remember where we are."

"Are you saying that it would be different if we were inside?"

"No. I'm not saying that at all. I'm saying that we might be seen," she said, swallowing nervously.

His eyes were full of macabre enjoyment. "And you don't want me to overlook the fact that you aren't wearing a bra?"

Her blush was more apparent than her voice was audible as she said, "I didn't think it was that obvious."

His gaze moved down from her face. "It isn't. It was a good guess. It would be interesting to follow this through." She felt his fingers leave her neck, the rope

fastening of her sundress still intact, with so much relief
that she felt dizzy. In a clipped voice he added, "It's
futile to contemplate the matter further, because I
don't have the time. I'm running late as it is."

His words had the advantageous effect of rousing her
from her malaise and replacing the look in her eye with
one of curiosity.

"I have a meeting set up which could take time.
Within reason, you're free to do what you want. That
should please you, knowing that I won't be around to
bother you."

She made a point of looking down at her hands to
conceal the disappointment she knew would show on
her face. Contrary to what he thought, she was quite
dismayed at the prospect of a day of freedom. She had
hoped he would suggest a delay in starting work
because she was eager to see something of her surroundings before getting her nose down to the grind-
stone. But she had anticipated Paul's being with her to
show her the sights. Good things should be shared, and
a day on her own, sightseeing and generally loafing
around, had little appeal.

"Don't start dinner without me," he instructed. "I'll
be bringing a guest back with me, possibly more than
one, and I want you to be present. Wear something
stunning. I want you to look especially good."

Feeling irritated by his manner, and the implication
that she was to be shown off like a prize trophy, which
surely didn't fall within the terms of her job description, she assented with marked reluctance. "All right."

His eyes narrowed at the stiffness of her tone, but all
he said was, "How will you spend your day?"

"Getting my bearings. And I still have to unpack."

"Ah, yes! Thanks for the reminder. Don't unpack."

Her dismay of a moment earlier was nothing to the
sinking feeling she experienced at his words. Yet again

her pride came to her rescue as she inquired, "You're sending me back home?"

She'd said the wrong thing again. It seemed that every time she opened her mouth she brought his vengeance down upon her head.

She was grabbed by her upper arms and yanked violently out of her chair. "You look as innocent as a newborn kitten, but you're as cunning as a cat. I brought you here for a specific purpose, and you're damn well going to fulfill it. I've told you before and I'll tell you again, and I'll keep on telling you until it sinks in. This time you've picked the wrong guy. No cheap little trickster is going to cheat on me. I've shelled out good money. I intend to get full value."

"That's fine by me." She wasn't a shirker. The check he'd given her in advance, the balance of which she'd banked for Ally to draw on for the needs of the business, had been extremely generous and she had every intention of working hard to earn it. "All this aggravation, simply because I asked if you were sending me home! What was I to think when you told me not to unpack?"

"I thought it might have occurred to you that New Providence was merely a stopping place before moving on."

"It might have crossed my mind, but I didn't know."

"I assumed you did."

"How could I?"

"You read the gossip columns, I presume? My private life has been chewed over pretty thoroughly in the past and there's been a recent revival of all the mud-slinging and the innuendoes. I find it difficult to believe that you missed it. I think you're putting me on."

"No, I'm not."

He was still holding her by the arms and although

their bodies weren't touching, she was too close—or not close enough—for comfort. She could feel the heat he was giving off, and her own body was no better behaved. The clean, masculine smell of him excited her. She had only to be near him to feel a prickly sensation in her fingertips which knew a terrible desire to reach out and touch him. She knew she should fight against these new and disturbing emotions, but she did not know how this could be accomplished. And it seemed unfair that she had to resist when she suddenly felt so alive. He had awakened responses in her that she hadn't known existed.

Enough! She must stop making excuses for herself, stop looking for justification. These were animal instincts which must not be allowed to get out of hand. And that led her naturally into thoughts of the vulnerability of her position, which was getting more complex all the time. She was away from home, heavily indebted to him and dependent on him for food and shelter. She had brought extra travelers' checks with her, to cover the unexpected, and she had more than enough to pay for her return ticket home. Should she make a run for it, before she got deeper in his debt, before Ally had time to draw on the money deposited in the bank? Yes, that would be the sensible thing to do—today, while he was away! She must pray that she could get a flight at such short notice.

Could he actually read her thoughts? She could hardly believe her ears when he said, "You can forget that." He towered above her, his face, excitingly handsome in fury, menace sparking from his jade green eyes, showing no compassion for the abject helplessness expressed by her pallor. It flashed through her tormented mind that it gave him pleasure to have her pliant and subservient to his will, because a smile, hard and without humor, lifted the corners of his mouth.

"You should have taken your chance to back out when it was offered to you. It's too late now. You made a bargain; I intend to see that you stick to it. I'm keeping you with me for as long as it amuses me to do so."

"You can't make terms like that. It's barbaric."

"I can and I am. I've paid liberally for that right."

"That's nonsense. You're talking as if you've bought me."

"And haven't I?"

"Certainly not! The days of buying people are over. You only bought my services."

"It amounts to the same thing," he said with arrogant and cruel indifference to her feelings, the contempt in his eyes puzzling her even as it stripped her of dignity. His voice took on a note of steel command.

"Remember what I said, *within reason.* Enjoy your day, but no tricks. Don't get up to any mischief, and don't get in touch with your man-eating companion from the plane."

"You can't dictate to me like this!" she said. But she had been too choked up with annoyance and humiliation to get the words out quickly enough to serve any useful or valid purpose. By the time she had summoned up her protest it was too late—he'd already left and she found that she was speaking to herself.

Chapter Six

She leaned her elbows on the balcony rail, ostensibly looking down, but not seeing the colorful scene 'round the swimming pool area, or the swaying casuarinas and coral sand lapped by the sea. All she could see was Paul's face, set hard in contempt and determination.

The man was a nut case, and her brain couldn't be working to normal capacity or she'd take no notice of what he said and catch the next plane home. But if she did it would be the end of Allycats, leaving them in a worse plight than before. Her mistake in accepting the commission would cost dearly. She would have to recompense Paul for the clothes she'd bought for the trip and her air fare, and she had no guarantee that Ally hadn't already drawn on the money she'd deposited in the bank. Even if Paul agreed to give her time to pay off the debt, it wouldn't solve everything. She felt that it had been her misjudgment, not Ally's, so she should be the one to pay. But would Ally let her? Knowing Ally, she'd insist on sharing the burden, and Ally had enough on her plate as it was. A blow like this could tip the balance; she might decide to give up the struggle to keep Samantha and let Ray's parents take control—in Samantha's best interest. But it wouldn't be, and Catherine knew without a shadow of a doubt that it would break Ally's heart to have to give up her daughter. A deep sigh escaped Catherine's lips. All things considered, she couldn't back out. It seemed that she was stuck with Paul, with his roaming hands and condemning looks and sharp tongue, and his undeniable magnetism and charm. Had he been repulsive she would have stood a much better chance of fending him off. As it was . . .

She still couldn't get over his cheek in thinking he could get away with such monstrous behavior. She had been right about him from the beginning. Feminine worship had ruined him. He was so used to women falling over backward for him that he was stunned when one held out against him. Like an overly indulged child, he couldn't bear to be thwarted. She could think of no other reason for his strange manner toward her. It was pathetic, really. She hadn't ever considered herself to be a head-turner, the type that left men gasping. At best, he must see her as some kind of challenge merely because of the indifference she was clinging to by the skin of her teeth. Once he overcame her scruples she would have no further attraction for him, and what kind of mess would that leave her in? As if she didn't know! She had never before met anyone quite like him and she could only rue the day that some perverse mischance of circumstance had put her so completely in his power.

Oh, well—nothing was going to be solved by futile repining. She might as well make the best of her unexpected day off and take a look 'round. Not being the type to find joy in lounging around swimming pools, she dug out a comfortable pair of walking sandals.

Before leaving the hotel she bought a postcard for Ally, which she filled out, tongue in cheek, in the lobby. Just a few hastily written lines to say that she'd arrived safely and all was well. She left it to be mailed at the reception desk, and then swung out the hotel door and made for the heart of the shopping area.

She looked in awe and admiration at the exquisite workmanship that had gone into making the popular crafts: straw goods, wood carvings and shellwork. She wandered into a courtyard where paintings and pottery were for sale, along with bolts of fabric in colorful island designs. She didn't buy anything, although the temptation was great, feeling it wiser, in the circumstances, to save her money.

Inevitably, the crush and the heat, her policy not to buy and her love of the sea drove her down to the beach. It was cooler there, but the heat was still overpowering. She succumbed to the appeal of a long, ice-cold, refreshing fruit drink, which she purchased from a beach bar, and soaked up the stunning difference of everything.

She had always thought that the sky was the same everywhere, a little bluer in some places, grayer in others. But this sky bore no relation to the sky back home. Nor did anything else about the place. The trees were different; the birds were different; the flowers were different. Even the air didn't smell like air as she knew it. It came pure on the wind, washed clean by the miles of ocean, and she would have been perfectly happy just standing there, breathing it in all day.

She saw Joseph, the Bahamian porter at the hotel, and she waved to him. He grinned back at her. His face reflected his way of life and exhibited the same look of contentment she had noticed on the faces of all the locals, a look which the holidaymakers hoped would rub off onto them.

She was enchanted by it all. The color, the atmosphere, the fringe-topped surreys drawn by horses wearing straw hats. One stopped, spilling out a boisterous, rowdy threesome. Two boys, clean-cut individuals in their early to middle twenties, one dark-haired, the other a ginger nut, the freckles on his laughing face burnt deep into his skin. And a girl, a tall, voluptuous blonde wearing tight-fitting pale blue pants and a twist of material supplying minimum coverage up top, who yelled, "Catherine!"

Simultaneously, Catherine greeted her in spontaneous delight. "Deirdre!"

"This is Piers and this is Jock and they're both fantastic guys, sweetie, so you can't go wrong."

"Let her make up her own mind," the dark-haired boy, obviously French and therefore Piers, said in accented English. "She can go wrong any time she wants to with me. *Enchanté*," he said, bending over Catherine's hand and sliding her a look of warm familiarity.

"Naughty boy, Piers," Deirdre chided with a giggle. "Catherine's not like that."

"You stick with me, Catherine," Jock said. For all his fiery hair his Scottish burr was soft and full of charm.

Catherine had no intention of sticking with any one of them. She suspected that they had been drinking. At least, Deirdre and Piers had; Jock seemed sober enough.

"We've had the most fantastic time," Deirdre said, tugging Catherine's arm and commanding her attention. "We've been to the Queen's Staircase—sixty-five steps hewn out of coral rock to provide swift passage for the troops from the fort to the sea. That's history, Catherine. Isn't it something! The queen was Charlotte, wife of George the third. And that's enough culture for one day. Now we're going for another little drink. Why don't you come with us?"

"Thanks, but no. I've just had a drink, and I don't want another."

"Now let me guess what potent concoction that would be," Deirdre said irrepressibly. "Water laced with water?"

"Fruit juice, actually. That's what you ought to be drinking."

"Oh, don't be so stuffy," Deirdre said, tossing her blond head. "I'm on holiday. If you can't let go a bit on holiday, what's the point in coming? Do yourself a good turn, kid; join us and have some fun."

It wasn't Catherine's idea of fun at all, but she thought she might have it on her conscience if she let Deirdre go off with the two boys by herself. They looked harmless enough, even the hot-eyed Piers, because she thought there was a lot of bravado in his attitude, and Jock seemed quite steady. On the other hand, Deirdre had only just got there, so she couldn't know them very well. Perhaps, Catherine decided, she'd tag on for a while and see what happened.

When they passed the beach bar she thought they'd forgotten they were going in search of a drink, and didn't bother to remind them. It never occurred to her that they were going farther afield in pursuit of their quarry, and she was surprised to find herself being taken to the landing stage, where a launch was tied up which they seemed to have a proprietorial interest in.

"Is this your boat?" Deirdre inquired.

"Not ours by right of ownership, worse luck," Jock admitted. "It belongs to our boss. Come on, girls. Let's have you aboard."

This was obviously for Catherine's benefit, as Deirdre needed no persuasion.

As Catherine hesitated, Deirdre giggled impishly. "The boys promised to take me for a run in her."

"Don't you fancy that?" Piers turned to Catherine and asked.

She did. It appealed to her immensely. A trip out to sea sounded like heaven. She couldn't think of anything she'd like better. It would be cooler away from the land and the prospect of feeling the clean sea air blowing on her face was an irresistible temptation. The launch was new and of the luxury class. The fact that the boys' employer had entrusted them with it surely had to be a recommendation of their characters. Their boss had to think they possessed a high sense of responsibility.

But still something held her back; some tiny nucleus of doubt made her hesitate. Something niggled, a scruple yet to be overcome.

It was ironic that Deirdre should find it and say with taunting accuracy, "Afraid that gorgeous hunk of man you work for might object? I know he wasn't very taken with the idea of your chumming up with me. That stood out a mile. I wouldn't be at all surprised if he hasn't banned you from seeing me. That's it, isn't it?" she squealed in triumph when Catherine wasn't quick-witted enough to deal with the look of dismay that came to her face at Deirdre's spot-on assessment of the situation.

"He said nothing of the sort," Catherine declared with bravado, but because it didn't come easy to her it was a weak lie and merely served to widen Deirdre's grin.

"I don't believe you," the blond girl challenged.

"Even if he did sort of hint at something of the sort," Catherine admitted unhappily, "you don't think I'd allow him to dictate what I do or who I see in my free time, do you?"

"I won't know that," Deirdre said slyly, "until I see whether you get on the boat or not."

It didn't help to notice that Jock and Piers were watching with amused speculation. Feeling outmaneuvered, not to mention annoyed with herself for aiding and abetting Deirdre and the boys by talking herself into trouble, Catherine knew she couldn't show herself to be spineless by walking away. With her chin held high, in direct contrast to the sinking sensation that she felt inside, she gave her hand to Jock and allowed him to assist her onto the boat.

Taking her place beside Deirdre, Catherine shrugged her shoulders in a gesture expressive of, "I'm here now, so I'll make the best of it."

Piers took the controls, opening up the throttle as they cleared the jetty with a roar of sound that attracted attention from the shore. Catherine wondered if one of the lifted heads belonged to Joseph and if he would let it slip to Paul that he'd seen her going out to sea in a launch with a blond girl, whom Paul would immediately identify as Deirdre, and two men. Too late to bother about that now, she decided philosophically. In any case, the exhilaration of riding the waves, feeling the wind whipping her hair into a streaming pennant, was so wonderful that it overrode her stirrings of unease.

Deirdre left her seat to stand by Piers and was immediately invited within the circle of his arms to take the wheel, which she did with alacrity. Catherine was duly asked if she would like a turn, but she declined, saying she was happy where she was—savoring the beauty all around her, watching the swirling folds of blue, aquamarine, green and crystal water frilling in their wake. Or looking to where the brilliant blue ocean burst into waves of white spume upon the glistening white beach of yet another islet or cay floating like a mirage in a shimmering heat haze.

Catherine was staring enthralled at just such a spectacle of delight, a crescent-shaped island with swaying mop-head palm trees and bleached white sand, when Piers pointed to it, announcing, "That's it. Won't be long now."

What did he mean? It was obvious that he was turning in to land.

"That isn't New Providence," Catherine protested.

"Who said it was?" Piers replied. "It's Coral Cay."

"So why are we stopping here?"

This time Deirdre answered, leaving Catherine in little doubt that she'd been in the know from the beginning. "Their boss has a house here. Isn't that the most fantastic thing? Imagine anyone being well oiled enough to own a retreat like this!"

Catherine refrained from commenting on that. She was too busy wishing she'd asked more questions at the onset. "Who is their boss?"

"Gus Strindberg, the film producer," Deirdre said with awe in her voice. "Don't be a wet blanket, Catherine. Don't spoil it for me."

Deirdre had a dreamy look in her eyes, that caused Catherine some dismay. Did she hope to be spotted? Deirdre had seen too many movies. Didn't she know that stardom didn't come that easily? Things like that just didn't happen in real life.

"Deirdre, I don't know for sure what's going on in that head of yours, but—"

"Don't start preaching, for goodness' sake," Deirdre cut in petulantly.

"I won't, if that's how you feel. But I do think you could have told me where we were going. I thought you were only going for a drink. You sprang the boat trip on me, and now this."

"It was put to me in much the same way. Piers and Jock asked me if I'd like to go for a drink. I said where. They said first we'd go for a spin out to sea if I fancied it, and on the way back call in at their boss's for a drink. All perfectly square and above board. Nothing at all underhanded, if that's what you're suggesting. You're too suspicious, Catherine," she chided. "You want to watch that. It's not a very nice character trait, and it's not fair what you are trying to do. You seem determined to spoil my day. Ordinary people don't get chances like this every day of the week and you should think yourself lucky you're included, instead of dropping insinuations all over the place and looking horribly wronged."

"I'm sorry," Catherine said in contrition. Feeling that up to a point Deirdre's criticism of her was just, she tried to inject a bantering note into her voice. "I see that it's my own fault I'm here. When you invited me to come for a drink with you I should have done what you did—asked where."

It worked. The atmosphere lightened miraculously and Catherine didn't even seem to be carping as she asked, "What time will we get back to New Providence?"

"Are you in any particular hurry?" Piers questioned casually, sending her a smile of Latin charm.

"I'd appreciate it if you'd get me back to my hotel in time for dinner." That way she wouldn't be missed. She wasn't exactly afraid of what Paul would do if he found out, it was just that it would be less unpleasant if he didn't.

Catherine told herself that Piers didn't answer because he needed every scrap of concentration to dock the boat. He even sent Deirdre away. "Be a good girl and go sit down. I mustn't have any distractions now, *chérie*."

Even Catherine's inexperienced eye saw that there was no natural harbor and that entry to the island, which at first glance seemed to be totally inaccessible by boat, surrounded as it was by the razor-sharp coral of the encircling reef, was negotiated through a narrow channel, a task which took up every last particle of Piers' expertise.

The maneuver was completed and they were safely inside; then Piers spat out something in French that sounded suspiciously like a swear word. Following the direction of his gaze, Catherine realized that it was the helicopter parked by the side of the house that was responsible for his agitation.

Jock's mouth gaped in dismay. "What's the chopper doing here?"

"Obviously there's been a change of plan," Piers replied tersely.

Deirdre's head jerked back and she inquired urgently, "What are you getting into a stew about?"

"Nothing—nothing we can't handle," Piers said, his smile back in place. "With a bit of cooperation from you."

"Cooperation? Doing what?" Deirdre asked, a puzzled frown coming to her face.

"Doing nothing. Keep quiet and do nothing, and perhaps you won't be seen."

"What do you mean by that? Seen by whom?"

"The boss. Gus Strindberg, of course."

"But you said you'd introduce me to him," Deirdre spluttered. "You *promised.*"

Piers shrugged his shoulders. "Shame on me. A little white lie, *chérie.* What you call bait to get you to come."

Catherine thought that it was about time she added a word. "Would you mind explaining what's going on?" she demanded coolly.

"I should have thought that was obvious," Piers replied insolently, without apology. "Little Miss Star-Struck here thought she was going to meet the famous movie producer who would take one look at her magnificent body and wave a big fat contract under her pert little nose."

"Only he wasn't supposed to be here," Catherine supplied flatly.

"Correct. We took him to New Providence this morning. That's what we were doing there. He had a meeting with the man who's directing his next picture and the two leads, and he was staying overnight. Our instructions were to pick him up in the morning. As we understood it he was bringing the director and his current girl friend and the two stars back with him."

"It doesn't have to be Mr. Strindberg who's hired the helicopter," Jock put in hopefully. "Does it?"

"Cut it out, Jock. Who else would it be?"

"I don't know. I guess you're right."

"You can't win 'em all, Jock. It's just rotten luck that something's happened to bring him back ahead of time."

"Rotten luck for you," Catherine said. "I'd say that his unscheduled return could be a fortunate turn of events for us."

"Mmm?" Piers smiled contemplatively. Catherine hadn't trusted him from the beginning, but every time she glanced his way in suspicion, he had been adept at covering up. Now that the game was up he had no need to disguise his thoughts. His eyes washed over her and his voice was silky and deliberately sensual. "A matter of opinion, *ma petite.*"

"You lousy swine!" Deirdre screamed at him, having only just found her voice again after the shock she had received.

"What language, *chérie,*" Piers tut-tutted. "I'm sorry that I set out to fool you, but I swear you wouldn't have been too disappointed. You would have had a good time, with no lasting harm done. I'm confident that you would have enjoyed it, if it hadn't misfired."

"Turn this launch 'round," Catherine demanded with more authority than she felt. "Take us back to New Providence this instant."

"Alas, that is not possible," said Piers. "Not until I've found out what is going on. Much as I'd like to help, this is the best position I've ever had. Good food, no shortage of women, an excellent wine cellar, perfect surroundings—all the bounties a man could wish for, in fact. Much as I would like to accommodate you, I cannot jeopardize all this by doing what you ask."

"You should have thought of that before you brought us here. Let me tell you—"

"No—let me tell you. You are going to lie low while we find out what this is all about. If you are good girls and make no trouble for us, we'll come back and take you to New Providence. O.K.?"

It was far from okay, but she couldn't make Piers take them back straight away, and they certainly couldn't swim back. Unsatisfactory as it was, she accepted the deal, bypassing Piers to entreat Jock not to be too long. Jock's vague nod of agreement was hardly confidence-inspiring.

When the two boys had ambled off, Deirdre said sheepishly, "You were right to be suspicious. I've been such a fool, thinking I was going to get an introduction to Gus Strindberg and kidding myself that something would come of it. A proper chump I've turned out to be, falling for a set-up like that."

She looked so helpless and down in the dumps that Catherine hadn't the heart to be cross with her. "You're too vulnerable for your own self-preservation. We both are."

Deirdre nodded in agreement. "They never intended to take us back tonight. It really grates on me what I could have got you into. I don't trust Piers now. Will he . . . do you think he will get us back tonight?"

"My life won't be worth living if he doesn't."

Deirdre bit heavily on her lip and said in deep repentance, "I'll keep my fingers crossed for you. No one's going to think it strange if my bed at the hotel is unoccupied tonight, but I can see your predicament. It won't be so hot for you to have to account to that dishy boss of yours."

"You don't know the half of it. Paul has a guest, or guests, coming to dinner. He made a special point of telling me to be there. If I'm not, he'll skin me alive."

Deirdre laughed weakly. "Paul—what did you say his other name was?"

"Hebden."

"Hebden . . . Hebden," she said to herself. "Has there been some mention of him in the press fairly recently? The name rings a bell."

"Funny you should say that. I haven't seen anything myself, but he mentioned something of the sort, a reference to some unkind gossip which he thinks I've read."

"He's not connected with the film industry, is he?"

"No. He writes detective novels."

"It isn't the same guy, then." In an abrupt change of subject, Deirdre inquired, "Are we really going to sit it out here?"

"What do you have in mind? Storming the house, asking to see Gus Strindberg and demanding to be taken back?"

"No, I suppose not." A rueful smile came to Deirdre's lips. "Piers doesn't deserve any consideration. It's Jock I'm sorry for. For his sake we've got to give the other smart aleck a chance to redeem himself."

"My own sentiments exactly." Catherine sighed in ironic agreement, thinking what a couple of softies they were.

"I was thinking that we ought to see something of the island while we're here. It's the opportunity of a lifetime. I don't know whether I mentioned this to you or not, but Piers told me that *Edge of Paradise* was shot here. Did you see that movie? Gus Strindberg was the producer and it starred Zoe Sheridan and Jeremy Cain. He was already established, but it was her first starring role and brought her instant fame."

"Yes, I saw it and thought it was marvelously realistic. The best movie I've seen in ages. It held me on the edge of my seat for the entire time. Was it really filmed here?"

"According to Piers. I know his track record for telling the truth isn't so good, but he wouldn't have any reason to lie about that. He promised to show me the waterfall—you know, where Zoe Sheridan did the nude scene. She was sticky from being in the sea, so she had a quick look 'round to make sure Jeremy Cain wasn't there before she took her clothes off—only the rat sneaked up and caught her in the act."

"He didn't sneak up. He'd just fished her out of the sea, remember? He was protective toward her."

"It was his fault she was in the sea," Deirdre pointed out. "He crashed the plane on the reef."

"He followed her to the waterfall to make sure she was safe," Catherine insisted. "I don't usually like nudity on the screen, but it was so beautifully done, so natural, that no one could take offense."

"And Zoe Sheridan has such a superb body that it's a shame not to show it off," Deirdre inserted mischievously.

Unperturbed, Catherine maintained her defense. "The man who directed it must possess extreme sensitivity."

"And an eye for a beautiful body," Deirdre quipped irrepressibly.

"Oh—you! You're right about one thing, though. If *Edge of Paradise* really was shot here at Coral Cay, it would be a sin not to have a look at the place. I'd love to see the waterfall, and the cave where the big love scene took place."

"Superb acting, the critics said—except it was for real." Deirdre's eyes rounded in gleeful speculation. "Did you know that Zoe Sheridan was the director's girlfriend? I wouldn't be surprised if that wasn't what got her the part. She left him for Jeremy Cain. That must have been tough on him, directing all those steamy love scenes and knowing that the passionate clinches continued after the cameras stopped rolling. Not that you could blame her. That Jeremy Cain is some looker, with those big baby-blue eyes and that mass of tight toffee-colored curls. I'd go off the straight and narrow for him any day of the week.''

Catherine vaguely remembered reading some of the gossip at the time, but she had let it float over her head. She preferred to cling to the illusion of sweetness and romance portrayed on the screen rather than the crude reality that took place off it. The film had made a deep and lasting impression on her. It had opened with the two main characters flying in a light aircraft which lost its bearings in a thunder storm, and came down on the reef encircling an uninhabited island. Not that they had known it was uninhabited, of course, as they survived the coral fangs of the reef, as deadly as shark's teeth, to battle with the fierce undertow and, thanks to his persistence and superhuman strength, eventually wash up on the white sand. They had kissed—he told her that her mouth tasted of the sea—and she had declared herself too exhausted to walk a single step. So he had carried her up the beach to the sanctuary of a cave, where they made their home. The story had been about their struggle for survival in primitive, back-to-nature conditions, and their dawning love for one another, a love they fought desperately to deny because they both had left partners back in civilization. They spent six tortured months together in this earthly paradise before they were found. What made it especially heartbreaking was their decision to do the right thing and return to their lawful partners. Catherine had come out of the cinema with eyes that were red and puffy from all the tears she had shed. The film had won awards and accolades and become a box-office sellout, and because of public demand a sequel was going to be made called *Return to Paradise*. As the cast and crew were to be primarily the same, the dead gossip about the director and the two co-stars' love triangle had apparently been dug up again by the more sensational newspapers.

They set off, carefully skirting the house the boys had made for. It was a truly beautiful house, with pastel-colored walls which were almost obliterated under a clinging, climbing mass of overgrown vines and bougainvillea. Built on the lines of a Spanish *hacienda,* not the more usual type of colonial dwelling found in these parts, it was set in magnificently landscaped gardens, with several terraces dropping down to the sea, each terrace decorated with statuary. The trees blazed with the flutterings of numerous brightly colored birds; the gardens were an eye-catching display of flowers that gave off an overpowering scent and attracted butterflies of especial brilliance.

The first impression of Coral Cay was of a well-maintained luxury haven. They soon walked out of this into dense vegetation, the nature-run-wild setting of *Edge of Paradise*. It was so poignantly familiar that Catherine wouldn't have been one bit surprised to see a suntanned masculine hand drag back a trespassing branch to allow the dark-haired Zoe a relatively unscratched passage.

When the hand did reach forward to lift back a branch and Zoe Sheridan appeared on the path in front of them, admittedly not the character she had portrayed in *Edge of Paradise,* but an immaculately made-up creature with the indefinable gloss and poise of a superstar, Catherine's mouth fell open in stupefaction. Yet why, when she came to think about it later, she didn't know. Some of the scenes of the sequel would obviously be shot on the same location. Had filming started, she wondered, or was the star familiarizing herself with the surroundings she had supposedly lived in for many months?

Catherine pressed well back to give Miss Sheridan automatic right of way, and noticed out of the tail of her eye that Deirdre was doing the same thing. The courtesy gesture was acknowledged by the tightest and most begrudging of smiles as the actress regarded them with open curiosity. Her male escort showed equal surprise at the unexpected appearance of two unknown females, but a smile laden with charm graced his boyishly full, yet dangerously sensual, lips. His bright paintbox-blue eyes twinkled with delighted appreciation—but whether he was appreciating the two strange faces for their appeal or their stunned expressions was another matter entirely. He made a gallant little half bow and continued on his way.

"D–d–did you see who that w–was?" Deirdre gasped out.

Catherine knew that it wasn't the feminine face that had made her companion practically swoon in ecstasy and amazement. She nodded. "Yes, it was Jeremy Cain."

"Pinch me to see if I'm dreaming. I've seen Jeremy Cain in the beautiful flesh! And I was too dumbfounded to do anything about it! Oh, isn't he lovely? A million times more handsome than he is on the screen. This must be the best day of my life."

Catherine laughed, feeling some of Deirdre's joy rubbing off on her and saying that it certainly was a day for surprises, little knowing as they began to walk again, drawn by the rushing sound of water falling from a great height, which presumably would turn out to be the waterfall in the film, that the biggest surprise was yet to come.

He was squatting on his haunches. The furious, full-bubbling noise of the water had blanked out the crackle of twigs underfoot as they stepped into the clearing. Some sixth sense must have alerted him to their presence. He stood up, turning 'round very slowly.

As jade green eyes met sapphire blue ones, surprise registered on only one face—hers. But this didn't occur to Catherine until very much later. Her stunned brain digested the fact that even though she had a slight time advantage, surveying him as she had for those few unobserved seconds, Paul was the one to keep his cool.

Chapter Seven

"Catherine," he said. Unruffled, outwardly pleasant, if with an underlying displeasure which was very apparent to her, master of himself and the situation. "What are you doing here?"

"Hello, Paul. I was just going to ask the same of you."

"There is a subtle difference. I don't have to account to you."

Whereas she did have to account to him, she thought hollowly.

"I came with . . . with Deirdre," she submitted lamely, remembering all too vividly his parting command not to get in touch with Deirdre, her "man-eating companion of the plane."

"Obviously," he said.

She swallowed, feeling ridiculously chastened as his eyes flicked scathingly over her. She hadn't deliberately set out to disobey him; she had stumbled on Deirdre by chance and had felt the need, in Deirdre's best interest, to accompany her on what had turned out to be a foolish and irresponsible escapade, although she didn't think that would rate as an excuse with him. In any case, she wasn't the type to blame someone else or make excuses. Neither was she going to go feminine and simper all over him—beg forgiveness with eyes full of appeal and supplication, or apply any of the little-girl tricks a lot of women were prone to call upon in a tight spot. Dissembling, likewise, was out of the question. So she straightened determinedly, assumed what she hoped was a confident tone and said truthfully, "Piers and Jock brought us in the launch, without first getting their employer's permission, I regret to say. It was their bad luck he came back unexpectedly."

"One person's quick thinking can be another's bad luck," he said obscurely.

"Is that a quotation?" She hadn't heard that one before.

"Shall we say a suitable comment? What did you have in mind to do now?"

"Keep out of the way until they can take us back."

"Presumably without Gus being any the wiser?"

"Yes," she said.

"But now the cat is out of the bag," he said.

"Apparently so."

She wondered if he was making a joking reference to the shortened version of her name. But his face was deadly serious, his tightly held mouth devoid of amusement as he said, "The only course, as I see it, is to make our way to the house and instruct Cleopatra, Gus's housekeeper, that there will be two extra for lunch."

Catherine was conscious of Deirdre's joy; the other woman's expression was a bright burst of inquiry and anticipation and it wasn't difficult to guess that she was speculating about whether Jeremy Cain would be present. It was also blatantly obvious that, in view of this new turn of events, she didn't care a bit that their discovery would earn Piers and Jock a reprimand for taking advantage of their employer's absence and bringing the two women over in the launch. Mr. Strindberg might even consider dismissal to be just punishment for their breach of conduct.

Under the circumstances, it was the height of irony

for Catherine to care what happened to them. Their misdemeanor could have had—could still have, judging by the severity of Paul's face—serious consequences for her. It was ridiculous to feel any responsibility at all, but she did. In the first place, she ought to have talked Deirdre out of it. Instead, she'd been bluffed into coming, having fallen for Deirdre's taunts that Paul wouldn't approve and not wanting to lose face. Paul did disapprove, but in an odd kind of way it was a benign censure, as if he knew she'd been outmaneuvered by Deirdre's deviousness. If she spoke up for the boys it would make it look as if there had been no coercion and point to her total involvement.

Sighing at her own stupidity, she said, "Paul, have you any influence with Mr. Strindberg?"

"What if I have?"

"Would you consider using it to square things for Piers and Jock?"

"I might, if I had a good enough reason."

"Would my asking you rate high enough?"

"Ungallant as it sounds—no. I must own to having a more self-indulgent reason than that in mind."

If only she knew what was behind that secretive, twisted smile. It was a front, she knew that. She wasn't naive enough to think she would get out of this lightly. At the same time, she felt a disarming and touching wave of gratitude toward him for not reading her the riot act in front of Deirdre.

The narrowness of the path forced them to walk single file. Paul went first to lead the way, followed by Catherine, with Deirdre bringing up the rear. Suddenly Paul stopped walking. Turning to face Catherine, he said, "Consider it smoothed out for those two unworthy characters. I'll make it right with Gus."

With studied deliberation he reached forward to remove an errant strand of hair from her forehead. His hand descended by way of her cheek and remained on her chin, tilting it in a demonstration of familiarity that she sensed was for her benefit rather than Deirdre's. She had the strangest feeling that he was telling her something, indicating that she should behave in a certain way, accept his familiarity in exchange for his compliance in the matter of Piers and Jock. It didn't make sense to her, but even so, she knew she was right. She gave an almost imperceptible nod, which found approval in his eyes and secured her chin's release. Without knowing what she had let herself in for or why, she had just sealed a bargain.

Cleopatra, Mr. Strindberg's housekeeper, turned out to be a Jamaican woman in her mid-forties, with an ample girth and a wide white-toothed grin. She accepted the two extra lunch guests with neither fuss nor surprise, as if she were used to people appearing from nowhere without notice and took it in her stride. Of Gus Strindberg, or Zoe Sheridan or Jeremy Cain, for that matter, there was no sign, and so Paul took it upon himself to instruct Cleopatra to show the girls where they could wash their hands and generally freshen up.

She ushered them into a luxury bathroom and left them to it, advising that lunch would be ready in twenty minutes or so and that drinks would be served on the poolside patio when they were ready.

Running water into a pale mauve basin, Deirdre said, after looking 'round and making the predictable exclamation of awe at her surroundings, "I didn't realize you had such a cozy working arrangement with your boss or I would have kept my own greedy eyes off."

"It's not that cozy," Catherine responded wryly.

Deirdre prattled on. "I got the shock of my life when I saw him by the waterfall. What's he doing here?"

"I don't know. I've been wondering that myself. He

had a meeting fixed up with someone this morning. It looks as if it could have been with Gus Strindberg."

"Wow! What do you think they have to do with each other?"

"I've been thinking about that. It's occurred to me that it could be something to do with the sequel to *Edge of Paradise*. Perhaps Paul's writing the screenplay."

"How fascinating! And it sounds logical. Oooh!" she squealed rapturously, almost hugging herself in her bemused delight. "Isn't this the most incredible experience? I can't believe I'm going to have lunch in such a famous movie mogul's house. Drinks on the patio, Cleopatra said. Oh, do hurry up, Catherine!"

It was a confusingly large house, more like a mansion, and Catherine wondered if they would find their way all right. To her intense relief they did so without difficulty by the simple expedient of following the tinkle of glasses, the murmur of voices, and one frequent full-blooded laugh. It was the gusty and appreciative rumble of enjoyment that issued from Gus Strindberg's throat, they were soon to discover.

A big man with bold Nordic features and a fair complexion, he had a handshake that was as welcoming and hearty as his laugh. First it engulfed Deirdre's hand, then moved on to take Catherine's in a prolonged hold as his eyes fixed speculatively on her face, telling her that Paul had made a satisfactory explanation for their being here, but raising alarm in her at what he might have said.

"Welcome to my house," he greeted them with just the faintest trace of a Swedish accent.

He hadn't waited to be introduced, but had come forward on his own. Zoe Sheridan and Jeremy Cain waited more reticently for Paul to perform the honors, the latter introduction sending Deirdre into a paroxysm of delight under the former's cynical surveillance.

Deirdre was in her element and determined to push herself forward, Catherine noted with extreme embarrassment. Did Deirdre have to be so blatant? Zoe Sheridan was openly contemptuous of her. Paul's attitude was guarded, but she knew what he thought of Deirdre. Gus Strindberg and Jeremy Cain were pleasant on the surface, but Catherine sensed that one of them was demonstrating a host's politeness, while the other was playing up to a fan. She didn't realize until later that her prickly, protective anxiety on Deirdre's behalf had dulled her mind to other things it would have been as well to observe.

Perhaps it was her earlier conversation with Deirdre, along with the presence of the film producer and the two superstars, that did it, but the setting, the deep and comfortable and colorful loungers, the circular pool and the glass-topped table set with tall frosted glasses and a matching jug containing an interesting-looking concoction afloat with fruit, was reminiscent of a scene straight from a Gus Strindberg production. The point that didn't occur to Catherine at the time was that the theatrical aspect didn't end there, but that everyone present—with the exception of Gus Strindberg, who seemed perfectly natural—was acting a part. Deirdre was out to impress in the hope of being noticed. Jeremy Cain was oozing with his screen-image charm. Zoe Sheridan's laugh was falsely high and brittle as it escaped her sullen mouth. Catherine found herself unconsciously maneuvered into the role that Paul had scripted for her. He was being excessively familiar in his manner, suggesting a degree of intimacy they didn't share. The way his hand rested on her arm, his fingers drawing sensuous circles on her skin, his trick of adding bits to confirm things she said, combined to make their relationship look both close and long term.

Gus asked her if she'd had a good flight, and that opened the subject of flying.

"I sat next to this woman who went to sleep practically on takeoff and snored all the way," Jeremy Cain proclaimed.

"How could anyone fall asleep while sitting next to you?" Deirdre gasped, gazing at him adoringly.

Gus said, "My first wife talked in her sleep."

"Is that why you divorced her—guilty confessions?" Zoe asked. "If you talk in your sleep, Catherine, be warned of the danger."

"I've been told that I do," Catherine admitted.

"But only gibberish," Paul said lazily.

Catherine couldn't believe her ears. The liberties he had taken with her body in private paled into insignificance beside this. He had as good as announced to everyone that he had slept with her.

No one looked aghast or gave any indication that he had said anything untoward, so Catherine decided she must have misheard. It was possible. Her brain wasn't too clear. She had taken a long, thirst-quenching draught of the innocuous looking fruit juice, not realizing until she'd repeated the action several times that it was spiked with a combination of spirits. The others didn't seem to find it all that heady, possibly because they were more used to liquor than she was.

Over lunch Zoe's earlier petulance melted into a mood of pure scintillation. She was exquisitely beautiful. Catherine recalled that her abundance of silky raven hair had reached her waist in the film. At this precise moment it was plaited 'round her head to show off the perfection of her features. Her eyes were the color of dark oloroso sherry, resting frequently on Paul with a strange, unreadable expression in their mysterious liquid depths.

It was natural, because this was the site where *Edge*

of Paradise had been filmed, for Catherine's thoughts to dwell for a moment on the one who'd loved her, given her her big chance, and lost her because of it. She couldn't help thinking of the friction the shifting relationships during the making of the film must have caused, or to wonder what further pain the shooting of the sequel would bring.

"No sign of the director and his new flame," Deirdre made use of an opportune moment to whisper. "If you remember, Piers said they were to be among the party he was instructed to pick up from New Providence in the morning."

"Perhaps they couldn't alter their schedule to come a day earlier than planned," Catherine responded.

"A pity. It could have been quite amusing. I'd have given a lot to see how Zoe reacted to her ex-director-boyfriend's new live-in girl friend. And whether he was still in love with Zoe."

"Piers didn't say she was his *live-in* girl friend. You shouldn't assume such things."

"Grow up, Catherine. Their sort don't stop at holding hands and kissing. They always sleep together."

"That's their business. I'm glad they couldn't make it. I wouldn't want to get caught in the middle of a situation like that, and I'm surprised you would. He's suffered enough. I hope he's found someone who'll treat him better than Zoe did and that they're both hopelessly in love with one another. That would be one in the eye for Zoe."

The love scenes, although beautifully and tastefully done, had left little to the imagination. The director must have known every kind of agony directing his woman and her new lover through them. He wouldn't have been unaware of what was going on for long. How must he have felt? Catherine wondered. And now— could he bear to watch the finished product and know that it wasn't just a brilliant piece of acting? How could he bring himself to go through the torture again by signing up to direct the sequel? She knew that a lot of exaggeration took place for publicity purposes, to draw the crowds, but the sequel was predicted to be even more daring and frank than the original had been.

After lunch everyone took advantage of the reclining loungers until it was agreed that the food had settled and more energetic pursuits could safely be allowed.

Someone suggested a dip in the pool, upon which both Zoe and Deirdre divested themselves of their clothes to disclose swimming apparel. Zoe's was so minute, a contraption of the scrappiest piece of material held together by a single, string-thin long lace, that even Deirdre's predictably tiny bikini looked modest by comparison. Catherine would have felt nude parading around in either one. Then she recalled the waterfall scene in *Edge of Paradise*. Nudity before a mixed assembly was nothing new to Zoe. And in all fairness, Catherine had to admit that she didn't strike a provocative pose, but conducted her near-nakedness with grace and naturalness. Perhaps, Catherine wondered, because she was too thin to look sensuous? Had she lost weight since displaying her luscious all in *Edge of Paradise?* Her measurements then had been perfect. Zoe as she was now could never wear the "body beautiful" tag; she was positively skinny, her bust practically nonexistent. In fact, Catherine decided with a small, smug smile, the delectable Zoe looked better with her clothes on. She was shocked at the pleasure she derived from this because she couldn't ever remember harboring a jealous or catty thought about another woman. What was it about Zoe that rubbed her the wrong way?

A shadow fell over her. She redirected her eyes and

took in Paul's excellent physique. He had stripped off his slacks and his lean hips were clad in plain, no-nonsense blue swimming trunks. A silver medallion suspended on a silver chain encircling his strong masculine neck rested in the growth of hair on his chest, enhancing his deep teak suntan. Her throat constricted as her eyes took pleasure in the virile and very male picture he presented.

He lifted one foot, maintaining a steady balance, and nudged her thigh with his big toe. "What about stirring those lazy bones?"

His eyes strolled indolently down her throat; she wasn't able to stop the telltale swallow that told of her disturbed emotions; and their jade green depths contained a marked twinkle as they dropped to the area most marked by the rapid rise and fall of her breathing.

Deliberately keeping his gaze in that vicinity, he said, "Why don't you strip off and enjoy the fun?"

His surveillance was having a strange effect on her. The bodice of her sundress seemed tighter. She hoped it wasn't giving away the fact that she was still as she had been on the balcony at breakfast that morning, bra-less, and that she hadn't had the foresight to equip herself with a bikini underneath.

"I'm sure Zoe could be presumed upon to loan you something," he said, his grin teasing.

Her glance automatically went to Zoe in her almost-swimsuit, which in turn brought a mischievous smile to her own lips. "I won't bother, thank you."

There was the faintest suggestion of a taunt in his voice as he said, knowing full well that such an ambiguous remark would provoke her curiosity, "I don't know why it is, but it's always the same."

"What is?" she asked before she could stop herself.

His eyes finally left their seemingly fixed observation

point to slide across to indicate both Zoe and Deirdre. "The girl with the best body is always the one who leaves the flaunting to others who aren't as favorably endowed, those without or those too voluptuously with, and keeps her perfect statistics well hidden."

She had to smile at the way he'd summarized both Zoe and Deirdre, unkind as it was; the blush, part pleasure and part confusion, came when she'd sifted through his words and found the compliment for herself.

It got him nowhere. She wouldn't be talked into borrowing a swimsuit from Zoe and joining him and the others, and so he left her to her sunbathing.

She wished she were back at the hotel so that she could curl up in bed in her darkened room. The spiked drink, the intensely hot sun, which she was also unaccustomed to, coupled with insufficient food in her stomach, were making her feel queasy. She closed her eyes on the beating glare, wishing she'd had the good sense to choose a lounger within the bountiful shade of the house or the canopy of trees, but feeling too lazy to move. She realized she was shivering. How was that possible in this heat?

She wasn't conscious of falling asleep, only of waking up. The sun had moved 'round, granting one of her wishes, because she was now in the shade. She felt much better, only a little floaty, and now she was cold because she was in the shade and not because of any disability. She sat up, surprised to discover that she was completely alone. The pool area was deserted.

Wandering into the house to find out where everyone was, she came upon Cleopatra, whose mouth opened in the white-toothed grin which seemed almost to be her trademark.

"There you is, honey. I was just going to take

another look at you. Last time you were out like a li'l babe in lullaby land. Like me to show you where you's sleeping? Will you be wanting a double room or two singles?"

"Aren't we returning to New Providence today, then?"

"No'm. The arrangements are for you to stay here, and I've been told to fix you up. Singles or a double?"

Catherine would have preferred two singles, but she thought it would have to be a double. Knowing Deirdre's aptitude for getting into trouble, and wondering where Piers' sleeping quarters were and whether Jeremy Cain was also a house guest and not just paying a flying visit, she thought it might be best to keep Deirdre under her eye.

"A double," she said with conviction.

Then she speculated on whether similar thoughts had been skipping through Cleopatra's mind. A bright look of intelligence widened the woman's grin and the hastily smothered peal of laughter was definitely saucy.

"Yes'm, Miss Catherine. This way if you please." As they went up the stairs she asked, "Which side of the house do you want? You've got the choice of the sunrise or the sunset."

"I'm not fussy. It doesn't matter either way."

Again Catherine was rewarded with a flash of those perfect white teeth as the housekeeper replied, to puzzle her, "In that case I'll give you the sunset. More romantic." The accompanying laugh was distinctly ribald.

The room she was shown into was truly beautiful. Catherine left off pondering Cleopatra's strange manner to voice her delight and appreciation. It was huge, tastefully yet luxuriously furnished, cool and restful, with a long balcony, shared with the next room. The sunrise side would have the mountains; this side appealed to Catherine much more, as it had a view of the sea.

She couldn't think of a tropical sunset without thinking of Paul, how he'd been waiting for her to come out of the bathroom—had it only been the night before?—to show her her first tropical sunset, witness her enjoyment and share the precious moment with her.

She realized, after she'd let Cleopatra go, that she ought to have been more practical, asking things like where everyone was and what time dinner would be served. She didn't bother going after her, but stepped out onto the balcony. The air was as sensuous as perfumed velvet, the sea lagoon-calm and serene, the only sound the distant roar of the surf on the reef. The sun had begun its nightly slide; the color of the sky was changing. In her mind she was back on that other balcony, her shoulders pressing against Paul's muscular chest. She heard a step behind her. Had Deirdre come up? Reluctant to curtail her thoughts, and needing a few seconds to compose her face, she didn't turn 'round.

"Come and see the sunset," she called over her shoulder. "It's a sight not to be missed."

"Stop pinching my lines," a voice—not Deirdre's—said.

She spun 'round, not realizing that he'd crept up behind her, and the unexpected collision of bodies would have sent her reeling backward if he hadn't reached out to steady her.

"Paul! I didn't . . . expect . . . to see you."

"You mean not this soon?"

"I mean I didn't expect to see you here." This habit of walking into her room without invitation had to stop. "Where have you been?"

"Didn't Cleopatra tell you? I took Deirdre back to New Providence and while I was there I called in at our hotel to collect our luggage and check out. The maid repacked the odd things you had taken out of your case."

"Cleopatra didn't tell me. It must have slipped her mind."

"She probably assumed I'd mentioned it to you. You were asleep when we left. You knew we were moving on. As this was our ultimate destination, it seemed a pity to wake you and drag you off to New Providence only to bring you back."

With Paul standing this close it was difficult to assimilate the facts. "You said you took Deirdre back to New Providence?"

"That's right. Escorted her to the door of her hotel. She asked me to say her goodbyes and to tell you how much she enjoyed today and meeting you, and that she very much hopes your paths cross again some time."

"Deirdre didn't—" She swallowed painfully. "—return with you?"

"Why should she?"

"Oh, dear. I thought—" What would Cleopatra think of her, asking for a double and not two singles? Because it was now appallingly obvious whom she was sharing with. She remembered the housekeeper's smothered laughter and saucy appreciation when she'd said they'd have a double room, and *knew* what she had thought. Perhaps of even greater concern, what was *he* thinking? He'd been chasing her pretty constantly from the moment she arrived. Did he think he'd won her 'round to his way of thinking? What had she agreed to?

Paul touched a finger to her hot cheek. His eyes took in the distress and agitation in hers. "Hey, what is this?"

"When Cleopatra asked me if we wanted singles or a double, I assumed I'd be sharing with Deirdre. You *know* that."

"I know no such thing," he replied in biting, frightening fury. "Although, thinking about it, I don't know why I'm so surprised. It's typical of you. You've blown hot and cold since we first met. The big come-on followed by the door slam. Will you tell me what game you're playing?"

"I'm not playing any game. I think your familiarity is contemptible. You've taken things for granted that no decent man would."

"God Almighty! What things?"

"That you could—"

"You two having a fight?" Cleopatra called out to them, her face appearing at the balcony door. "I knocked. If you didn't want me to barge in on you, you should have locked your door. You knows I was coming to unpack your bags, Mister Paul; I did told you."

"That's right, you did," Paul said tersely, not looking at Cleopatra, but keeping his eyes fixed on Catherine. "I need to cool off. If you don't mind, I'll shower first."

His expression said that he wasn't skipping out of an argument, and he waited until she made a sign of assent before turning on his heel and slamming into the bathroom.

With Cleopatra looking at her with her big, anxious, disapproving eyes, what else could she have done but let him go?

"You giving Mister Paul a bad time, girl?" Cleopatra chided.

"You don't understand, Cleopatra."

"I understands enough. He's a good man and he's had it mighty rough. I can't figure out you modern girls. Mebbe your mommas didn't smack your bottoms often enough when you were li'l children."

"Cleopatra!" Catherine gasped in gentle remonstrance.

"I knows. Knows my place. My place is to unpack

your things and get back to my kitchen." She was still muttering to herself as she turned and waddled back into the room.

Catherine didn't want her clothes unpacked. Even though it was partly her fault, she had no intention of sharing a room with Paul. But she didn't follow Cleopatra to tell her so because she didn't think it was fair to involve the housekeeper in their private battle, and it wouldn't take her long to push her things back into her suitcase once the woman had departed. Also, if she were truthful, she was just a little bit scared of Cleopatra's candid tongue. It had certainly reduced her to size. That, coupled with the way Cleopatra had looked at her, had made her feel guilty when she had nothing to feel guilty about.

"All done, Miss Catherine," Cleopatra said, once again popping her head 'round the balcony door.

"Thank you, Cleopatra."

Now that she'd gone, Catherine went back into the room. On cue, Paul came out of the bathroom, a towel secured 'round his middle. He'd washed his hair. He raised a hand to push back its dripping wetness from his forehead.

"I'll dry off in here. You'd better take your shower. We're going to be late for dinner. Informality is the rule for the daytime only. Gus likes punctuality at his dinner table and for his guests to pay him the courtesy of dressing up. Bear in mind what I said to you this morning. Wear something special. I want you to be a knockout."

"I won't be displayed as though I'm part of your personal effects. I'm neither a trophy nor a chattel, and I won't be treated as such."

"You will," he said through gritted teeth. "That's little enough to ask."

She fumed, knowing that Paul's check had been

exceptionally generous expressly to cover the cost of a
new wardrobe to suit the climate and conditions. At the
time there had been an unspoken agreement between
them that she would do him proud. Now, though, she
objected most strongly to the crude connotation of his
words. While he was in the bathroom she had considered the possibility of having to put in an appearance
downstairs, and had mentally selected the floating
chiffon in shades of blue—the one Ally had convinced
her to buy. But instead she reached into the long fitted
cupboard where Cleopatra had hung her clothes and
defiantly stopped at another gown, still pretty but more
subdued, lacking the impact of her first choice.

Paul's hand stretched imperiously in front of her.
"Wear this," he commanded, holding her original
choice, the blue chiffon dress, out to her.

Her eyes blazed into his. "I will not be dictated to.
We're going to have to talk this out."

"I agree. You're not getting off this easily. But it will
have to wait until later. You are *not* going to embarrass
me by causing a spectacle in my friend's house. You will
put on this dress and we will go down to dinner and
make pleasant and inconsequential conversation, and
then we will come back up here for a serious discus-
sion."

The last thing she wanted was to cause a scene. In
embarrassing him, she would also embarrass herself.
Furthermore, she had eaten very little lunch and she
was hungry now. And since Cleopatra was in sympathy
with him, the girl who supposedly hadn't had her
bottom smacked often enough as a child wouldn't have
her supper sent up to her room on a tray, but would be
made to go without as punishment. It would be foolhar-
dy to continue the battle on an empty stomach. So she
accepted the dress from him and stormed into the
bathroom with it.

She knew that it suited her and she was glad that Ally had talked her into the extravagance of buying it. Its subtlety did not stop at the clever merging of blues, but also lay in its creation of a sensuous yet romantic image. It left her shoulders, throat, back, and quite a lot of her front bare, caressing her full breasts, scooping in to her tiny waist and drifting out 'round her hips as she moved. Up-to-the-minute stylish, yet hauntingly old-fashioned. Her color-matched evening sandals picked out two of the shades of blue and were sensationally high; she would need to walk carefully, but decided that the extra caution would be a small price to pay for the additional height she achieved. She applied her make-up with care, eye-shadow for a touch of mystery, lipgloss for shiny sensuality. In her present heated mood she didn't need blusher. As she stared critically at her appearance she knew that she couldn't do better, yet at the same time there was about her an underlying diffidence that gave her an appealing air of modesty and charm.

"I'm ready," she called out to Paul, who was on the balcony.

As he came toward her she wouldn't have been a woman not to look for his response. It was favorable, but not in a way she could accept.

"Enchanting! Adorable!" His eyes were gloating as they traveled over her; his breath was expelled with self-satisfaction and insufferable smugness. "I've never seen you look lovelier than you are now. A certain party, accustomed to having the limelight all to herself, won't be disposed to welcome such formidable competition. The others are going to look at you and envy me."

"That is the most pompous and ridiculous thing I've ever heard," she said, giving vent to her feelings. "No one's going to envy you a thing. They'll look at my temper-flushed cheeks and know we've been quarreling."

"On the contrary, precious heart," he drawled in amusement. "They'll look at the sparkle in your eyes, couple it with your *passion*-flushed cheeks, and think we've been making love."

Chapter Eight

Despite that disturbing observation, she got through the evening without finding it too much of an ordeal, her thoughts frequently absconding to sift and resift every word that had passed between her and Paul in an effort to make some kind of sense of his attitude toward her. She didn't like the way he made her feel that she was doing wrong by not letting him do what she knew wasn't right.

He had enough going for him in the way of looks, wealth and fame to have been spoiled by a certain kind of woman into thinking that all women would be willing to leap straight into bed with him, and he was piqued at her for resisting. But it wasn't only that. If it had been, she could have hardened herself, albeit with great difficulty, against the charm he was pouring on, which she knew was for the benefit of the others 'round the table. But she had a strange, persistent, uneasy feeling —a presentiment almost—that there was more to it than that, something she still had to uncover.

"I'm sorry," she said when Jeremy had to repeat something he'd said to her for a third time because of her inattentiveness.

"Too bad, Jeremy," Gus cut in. "This girl only has eyes for Paul." His distinctive, hearty laugh marked his appreciation of this rare occurrence. "Jeremy Cain, superstar, having to fight for a girl's attention!"

True, she had kept looking at Paul, but only in inquiry, to try to work out what this was all about and not because—well, not *totally* because—she found him distractingly handsome in formal clothes. The men all wore dinner jackets. Gus and Jeremy had opted for frills and embroidery in their choice of shirts with velvet cummerbunds, but Paul's more sober selection served him equally elegantly. In fact—

"I'm sorry," she had to say yet again, bringing her wandering concentration back to Jeremy, "I didn't quite catch that."

"You're a difficult girl to compliment, an unusual one, too. Until this moment I've always found that a sure-fire way of making a girl hang on to your every word is to tell her how charming she looks. Did you realize that there's one shade of blue in your dress which exactly matches your eyes?" Jeremy said, looking into them with barely a trace of rebuke.

"Oh, come on now!" Zoe interjected sourly. "That's clever feminine strategy. You didn't really think it was coincidental, did you?"

"Is someone's delectable nose feeling slightly out of joint?" was Jeremy's wry comeback.

"Now, children," Gus intervened. "I won't have bickering at my table. You look charming, too, Zoe."

If that was an attempt to placate the actress it failed abysmally, highlighting as it did Zoe's pettishness because another girl was getting noticed. Zoe had no cause to be jealous of the attention Jeremy was paying to her, Catherine thought. Anyone with a scrap of intelligence could see that he was only being kind to the stranger in their midst. No one could outshine Zoe, who was dramatically beautiful anytime, but who took one's breath away that evening in a pure white dress that complemented her golden suntan and black hair.

The meal over, Gus suggested they have their coffee

and brandy or liqueurs on the terrace. "You four go ahead. I'll see what's keeping the coffee."

Jeremy rose to pull Catherine's chair back for her, but Paul got there first, his fingers pleasantly proprietorial on her arm as he led her out to the moon-draped terrace. Gus, or someone, had put on a record and the strains of music to dance to followed them out.

Without asking her preference, Paul guided her past the tables and chairs. "Can you dance?"

"Uh-uh."

"In the old-fashioned way?" he asked, sliding her fully into his arms.

"Is there any other way?" she asked recklessly, not knowing what had got into her.

"You're like the cat who swallowed the cream," he observed. "Perhaps I should amend that to the kitten who swallowed the cream," he added after a pause.

That was just how she felt. Even if Zoe was looking daggers at her it was nice to be made to feel important and fussed over by three such attractive men, because even though Gus was playing a minor part when compared with the other two, he had still made her feel very welcome at his table.

However, modesty insisted that she take the cliché literally. "I am. That *Crème Brulée* was out of this world. And I've never tasted steak as delicious, although perhaps there was too much wine for my poor spinning head in the red wine sauce."

"*Entrecôte Marchand de Vins* is one of Piers' specialties."

"Piers? I thought I should compliment Cleopatra."

"Don't be fooled by all that 'back to the kitchen' talk. She may be a good housekeeper, with an attractive and amiable disposition, but she can't boil an egg."

Catherine pondered on that for a moment and then said, "If you heard Cleopatra say anything to me about getting back to her kitchen, you also overheard something else."

The devil himself was in Paul's smile. "You mean about Cleopatra scolding you for not treating me right? The island women have a wonderfully uncomplicated attitude toward sex and pleasing their menfolk. The man is the master and a woman should be grateful for the high regard he pays her by fancying her."

"And no doubt you agree with that?" she said, sarcasm and disapproval mingling in her tone.

"I do, most decidedly. Cleopatra talks a lot of sense." Again that smile. "You *would* have benefited by having your bottom smacked when you were a child. I have my own theory to add to that. It's never too late to repair a fault."

"Just you try!"

"Is that an invitation?"

"Get lost!"

"That's not a very nice way to show your appreciation for making it right for those two scoundrels, Piers and Jock, as you asked me to."

Her chin came up. "About that . . . it would be interesting to know exactly what you did say to Gus. How did you make it sound credible?"

"All that matters is that I did; I didn't exactly want to look a fool. A guy needs his wits about him to keep up with you. You are aware, I take it, that Gus and party were my intended guests this evening?"

"I thought they might be."

"Perhaps you'd tell me just how you proposed to get back to New Providence to be at the hotel in time for dinner? You knew I wanted you to be there. I said no tricks, remember? Did you go off to get back at me?"

"No. I didn't think there would be any question of my not being back in ample time. Deirdre, Piers and Jock led me to believe we would only be out at sea for the day. I didn't expect them to stop off here. If a trick was pulled, it was *on* me, not *by* me."

"I'd like to have been there to see the expressions on their faces when they saw the helicopter, put two and two together, and realized their little game had been scotched. I bet they got quite a shock."

She giggled. It hadn't been funny at the time, but she could look back and see the hilarity of the situation. "They did, as a matter of fact. I've felt sorry for Jock all along, because it's obvious that he's easily led, but I'm beginning to have a sneaking sympathy for Piers, as well. I caught a glimpse of him earlier on, as we came down to dinner. He didn't know where to look. He can't seem to take it in that I'm staying here as a guest."

"I think Piers will be more prudent in future," said Paul. "I'm not saying that he won't ever bring another girl over when Gus is out of the way, but next time he'll be more cautious in his selection. I could beat the living daylights out of him when I think about it. And I'm not too pleased with you, either."

"I know. Thank you for not telling me off in front of Deirdre when we came upon you at the waterfall, though. And thank you for smoothing things over for Piers and Jock."

"It was the least I could do, considering that I was the one who botched things up for them."

"You?"

His eyebrows lifted in incredulity. "You didn't honestly think my being here was a coincidence, did you?"

She nodded in embarrassment. "I must be even dumber than I thought, because yes, I did. I thought you turning up here was pure good fortune. Is that what you meant when you said one person's quick-thinking can be another's bad luck?"

"What else? When Joseph told me he'd seen you getting into Gus's launch, I knew that it would be most unlikely for me to see you back at the hotel in time for dinner. Having already told everyone about you, I wasn't going to be stood up. I had to do something fast."

"Joseph told you!" she said, frowning heavily. She remembered seeing the Bahamian porter and wondering if he would say anything to Paul, but she had decided that he wouldn't stoop to telling tales.

"It wasn't like that. Joseph didn't come racing to find me with a spicy piece of gossip. He came to tell me because he was worried and he didn't know what else to do. All the locals know what Piers and Jock get up to and he was concerned for you."

"I'm sorry I misjudged Joseph." She paused, then said, "You still haven't explained how you worked things out. Does Gus know how stupid I've been?"

"No. I concocted a tale about wanting to come here to get one aspect of the film fixed firmly in my mind before the crew arrives. Gus applauds dedication to duty and fell in with the change of plan. He's also a man of the world, so he wouldn't expect me to give up my comfort because of it. What more natural than for me to send Piers across in the launch for you? I explained Deirdre's presence by saying she just happened to be with you and came along for the ride. Satisfied?"

"Apart from being referred to as your comfort, yes. I wouldn't like Gus to know what a brainless idiot I've been. Looking back, I can't understand why I was so foolish. It wasn't a conscious decision, more like drifting into something without knowing what was happening. I'm sure that could never happen to you," she said with positive emphasis.

"At one time I would have agreed with you," he replied, frowning heavily, as if at a discovery he'd made, one he didn't much care for, but using a certain wistfulness of tone that created considerable pleasure in her heart.

On the whole, she thought, she'd come off rather well, even if it had been a bit like jumping out of the frying pan into the fire. At this precise moment, the fire was decidedly cozy.

During the latter part of the conversation their feet had stopped moving in time to the music, but he'd kept his arms 'round her. Suddenly one hand lifted to the back of her neck; the other slid down her spine, coaxing from her a smoldering response that came as a revelation. Flames burst inside her, igniting a sensuality she had been unaware of possessing. Her mind blanked out in shock; her body instinctively arched itself to his, promoting a closeness between them that she had never before known with any man, giving her intimate knowledge of the fact that she was not the only one awash with fire.

"You do pick your moments," he said groggily, bending his head to take her eagerly given lips, drawing hungrily of their sweetness as the hand on the small of her back pressed harder, making his whispered, "How much I want you!" superfluous. She had been trembling with the awareness of that before he murmured a single word.

"We'll have to join the others," he said in a smothered voice.

She was glad that one of them had remembered where they were in time, and also grateful for the patch of shade which Paul had thoughtfully drawn her into, even though it was no doubt obvious why he'd taken her aside.

She nodded tremulously, a throbbing alertness to every nerve and sensation in her body taking the power from her legs. Without his arm 'round her waist, assisting her progress, she never would have made it back.

"I was just going to shout 'cut,'" Gus said when they rejoined the others. "Your coffee's getting cold."

Catherine declined the brandy which Gus tried to press on her. She was tingling from head to foot as it was, and feeling quite good, she decided. Scared out of her mind, but good.

This would certainly rate as an evening to remember. At lunchtime, Deirdre's presence had done much to neutralize the undercurrents. Impressions were sharper in her absence. Deirdre had been *de trop,* not one of the essential characters. There she went again, Catherine thought, likening the situation that was unfolding around her to a stage play. But that was exactly how it seemed to her. Everyone knew their lines except her; she was the only one stumbling along, although not totally without direction. The feeling that she was being manipulated by Paul still persisted. Gus, she thought, wasn't a principal character, but he was necessary just the same. He was the audience the other characters needed to play off, a hugely appreciative audience, one who was finding it all highly entertaining. Zoe and Jeremy were the lovers—lovers in dissent, she gathered. Had they tired of each other, or was one simply retaliating to signs of boredom in the other? Jeremy had gone out of his way to be kind to her, had flirted with her. Perhaps it had been a form of self-protection, because he suspected that Zoe was reverting to type and getting ready to treat him as shabbily as she had her director boyfriend. Did he think he was soon to be cast aside in favor of some new distraction? Had she turned her thoughts to Paul? She had a way of looking at him, guardedly, from under lowered lids. Catherine knew from Paul's secretive smile that he was aware of it, even if, so far, he wasn't doing anything about it. Was it because he was astute enough to see through her? Did he know there wasn't one drop of sincerity in Zoe's entire system and that she was as false as the eyelashes she kept lowering at him, but in such a captivating way that Catherine wondered how long he would hold out?

Catherine's chair was next to Paul's. His tanned hand rested on the arm. Her own slid forward, obeying a compulsion, a yearning to feel his flesh against hers, wanting to cut Zoe out of his thoughts. Their little fingers brushed. Her wildest imaginings couldn't have foreseen the amount of feeling it was possible for a little finger to transmit. It brought her to her senses, to the realization that the fire wasn't cozy anymore. It was a raging inferno that would consume her if she allowed it to.

Her hand jerked back in alarm. She shuddered to think what would have happened if they'd gone immediately to their room after that explosive kiss. She thanked the blessed angel of convention that had forced them to observe the social laws and rejoin their host and fellow guests. She had been given time to come out of the sensual euphoria that kiss had induced. Knowing how easily Paul could arouse her, and to what dynamic effect, plunged her into panic. No way could she spend the night alone in a room with him. She must find Cleopatra and ask to be given a bed somewhere else. In a house this size there were bound to be plenty of empty rooms available.

The coffee cups had not yet been removed. She saw them as a means of skipping out and going in search of Cleopatra to make her request before it got any later. She stacked everything onto the tray, announcing, "I'll take these through to the kitchen."

"Don't trouble yourself with that," Gus said airily.

"No trouble," she insisted.

But when she got to the kitchen there was no joy, either. It was spic and span and deserted. She washed the crockery, dried each piece and put it back on the tray for someone else to put away. Still no sign of Cleopatra. She was just wondering whether to try to find her when Paul appeared at the kitchen door.

"You wouldn't be following me, would you?" she inquired, bristling as his long stride shortened the distance between them.

"We're out of ice. I volunteered to fetch it."

"Oh!" She sounded more defiant than chastened. "Do you know where Cleopatra is?"

His eyes narrowed, active and suspicious. "Why do you want her?"

"To ask for another room. I should have insisted on sorting things out before, when I found out it was you I was supposed to be sharing with and not Deirdre. But your arguments were very persuasive. I didn't want to cause a scene and embarrass you in front of your friends. But now I don't care if I raise the roof if that's what it takes to get it through to you that I am not spending the night with you."

She didn't realize that her voice had reached a high pitch of hysteria until he commanded, "Quiet. Unless you want the whole house to hear."

"I don't care if they do." She'd reached the point where she was past caring. "I will not be talked out of my convictions this time. You go too far. You do things to me you shouldn't."

"It takes two. What do you think you did to me earlier, out there on the terrace?"

She lowered her eyes. "That was ungallant. You made me like that. You're very adept at making a girl respond to you. I put that down to experience. You're an expert because you've researched the subject thoroughly."

"If you don't stop this, I'll do something else thoroughly. I'll tell you this much, in all this vast experience you credit me with having, I've never met a woman like you before."

She was saved the necessity of thinking up a reply by Cleopatra, who announced herself by calling out loudly from the kitchen door before coming right in. "Tell me, Mister Paul, do you two fight all the time, or do you save it up for when I'm about to bust in on you?"

"You do seem to have a knack for timing your entrances, Cleopatra," Paul said tightly.

The whites of her eyes flashed as Cleopatra shifted her gaze to rest momentarily on Catherine before returning it to where her sympathy lay. "That li'l gal sure is a pretty parcel of trouble for you, Mister Paul."

"Tell me something I don't know, Cleopatra. Did you want something?"

"Just to tell you that your room's ready. I put you next door to Miss Catherine, in the room that shares the balcony. In case you wants to make it up," she said, her eyes switching back to Catherine, giving her such a funny look, condemning yet at the same time appealing —presumably for Catherine to come to her senses.

There was a conspiracy against her! If she hadn't already felt victimized—the circumstances leading up to her finding herself in this predicament had been particularly capricious and unkind—she might have found it quite laughable. And then her impish sense of humor burst through to join her fury, so that despite the rising anger she felt toward Paul for knowing what he did and letting her babble on, the absurdity of the situation struck her and she had to quell a laugh. Perhaps it was just relief she felt, she thought, sobering at the grimness of Paul's expression as he thanked Cleopatra for organizing things, then explained what had brought him to the kitchen. "We need ice."

"You two go about your business. I'll bring the ice in," Cleopatra replied in her pretty sing-song voice, which slid naturally into a snatch of calypso. For all her size her step matched perfectly to the lilting tune as she moved toward the refrigerator.

As Paul took her elbow to guide her back to the salon, Catherine envied Cleopatra her easy and carefree temperament and wished she didn't have to make the apology that was sticking in her throat. She felt that Paul could have shut her up and spared her this embarrassment by telling her that he'd already approached Cleopatra about the matter that had been weighing so heavily on her own mind.

"Thank you for having a word with Cleopatra about you know what," she said gruffly.

"Think nothing of it."

"Oh, but I do!"

"Chivalry had nothing to do with it, if that's the mistaken impression flitting through your head," he replied in contempt. "I was being characteristically selfish. Seeing it as the lesser of two evils."

"Oh?"

"As I saw it, I could either throw myself at Cleopatra's mercy, risking her scorn, or if your determination was a reliable indication, contemplate spending the night on the balcony."

"I see," she said, trying to keep the skepticism out of her voice.

"After our dalliance on the terrace, however, I wondered if I should have bothered asking for a separate room."

"If you hadn't, it would have been the balcony," she

retorted, stepping ahead of him on her precariously high heels.

Just short of the door he reached for her fingers, holding them captive, his gaze dropping to the vulnerable curve of her mouth. She thought he was going to say something, but his eyes merely lifted to hers in frowning interrogation, the inquiry sealed in their jade green depths.

She still felt shaken by his appraisal as they joined the others for the tail end of the evening. The time was racing by, dinner having been served at a late hour. The sparkle had gone for her and she wasn't sorry when bedtime murmurings were made, yet each person seemed to be waiting for someone else to make the first move.

Finally it was Paul who levered himself from his chair, his eyes floating across to meet hers. "I'll escort you up, if you're ready?"

"I am," she responded gratefully. She rose and turned to her host. "Thank you for a wonderful meal, Gus." She had started out calling him Mr. Strindberg, but he had insisted that she drop formality. Because he was a very easy person to know, she had been able to do so without any self-consciousness.

"My table was enhanced by your delightful presence," he said with old-world gallantry. "Good night, Catherine. Sleep well."

"Thank you, I'm sure I will. Good night, Gus."

Zoe and Jeremy were also getting to their feet and in the general exodus the good nights continued up the stairs. Now that the humiliation of sharing a room was not to be forced on her and the fear of that intimacy had been removed, she didn't mind Paul taking a proprietorial hold of her hand, which fitted in his fingers as though it had been fashioned for that purpose. At her door it did not gain its freedom until it had been warmed by a gentle squeeze.

Then he bid her an airy, "Good night," and continued along the passage to the room next to hers, the one that shared her balcony, she remembered in discomfort.

She hoped he realized that "good night" was final. He turned his head at just that moment and caught her eyes on him, and immediately a trace of wry amusement lifted the corners of his mouth. It was as if he knew exactly what she was thinking and his smile mocked her prudishness and at the same time held a taunting threat that made her confidence ebb and brought hot color into her cheeks.

With a scathing lift of her chin and a determined straightening of her shoulders, she swept into her room, closing the door with a decisive bang.

Once out of his vision her hauteur left her. She sat down on the edge of the bed and wished that she were better able to cope. It was infuriating to feel so put out. Her original opinion of him still held, but with certain dangerous qualifying factors. He was everything she disliked in a man, yet she could not bring herself to dislike him. He was too assertive, and overconfident. It was supremely egotistical of him to think he was irresistible to all women. Perhaps not *all* women, she thought wearily, but certainly a high percentage would have difficulty in evicting him from their thoughts. It wasn't in the least comforting to know that, contrary to all the ardent disclaimers she had made to herself, she, too, was one of the women who found him devastatingly attractive and impossible to resist.

The knock on her balcony door, though not unexpected, made her jump. She would have preferred not to answer it, but realized that Cleopatra wouldn't have locked it, so if she didn't go he would probably come in anyway. And she could hardly be so juvenile as to jump up and lock the door herself, knowing he would hear the noise the key made as it was turned. Hoping to strike a compromise, she drew back the curtain and looked at him through the glass.

He held up a copy of his book, the copy she'd bought so she'd be able to say that she had read his work before applying for the job of typing his manuscripts. Even though Cleopatra had made it perfectly clear that she expected some to-ing and fro-ing, this had not been a piece of deviousness on the housekeeper's part, but a clear-cut and obvious mistake. Cleopatra would naturally have assumed that the book belonged to him and had removed it, with the rest of his possessions, from her room. He could have picked a more suitable time to return it, though, she thought, fuming as much as she was quaking at the blatant pretext for getting into her room.

She opened the door the merest crack, allowing just sufficient space for the book to be passed through. She didn't exactly reel back in surprise when he assisted it the rest of the way and boldly gained entry.

"The book was an excuse," he admitted, carelessly tossing it down on the bed. "I could have returned it in the morning. We have to talk."

"Talk?" she said with an eloquent lift of her brows.

Since she had seen him last he had removed his jacket and tie and he looked casually elegant in shirt sleeves. Several strands of hair had found their way onto his forehead. He pushed them back, his eyes too knowing for her peace of mind.

"Unless you've got a better idea?" he quizzed in lazy insolence.

"If you've got something to say, say it and get out of here," she said, her voice abrasive, despite the emotion that was making it difficult for her to breathe evenly.

"That's not very friendly," he chided, his smile as feigned as his indifference, encompassing his mouth only and not touching his eyes.

"There's a perfectly good explanation for that. I don't sound friendly because I don't feel friendly."

His face hardened and she knew that she had handled things all wrong. It was penetrating her shaking senses somewhat belatedly that she had misjudged his reasons for butting in on her at such a late hour. He'd said "to talk" and she hadn't believed him. Now, though her belief was too late to be of practical help, she did. There had been an affableness about his manner when he first came in which, as a result of her suspicions, had now gone.

"To be blunt, shouldn't you have worked out your feelings before taking on the assignment?" he said. It was a reasonable query, but asked in a cold, jarring tone.

She swallowed hard. "That's a fair question. Yes, I should." She had known all along that it was a difficult situation. As far back as the interview—even before that, when they had first met at Lois's party—he had made improper passes at her with his eyes. "I needed the money, desperately, for the survival of Allycats. I didn't think beyond that."

"That's honest, at least," he spat out contemptuously. Just before he'd spoken he'd given a small choked-back gasp, as though she'd said something to shake him. His composure, however, was not as lost as hers and he retrieved it without apparent effort, his features taking on a look of scorn that flicked her already raw nerves. "My only motive in pressing to see you was to put your mind at rest, to allow you to get a good night's sleep and wake up in the morning without worrying about what the day would bring. I've been weighing the pros and cons all evening, and I've finally decided that this was another of your unconscious decisions, that you got yourself into it without really appreciating what it was all about. But have a care, Catherine. I'm only human. Never in my born days have I met such a provocative bundle of mischief as you. Not only your tongue, but your body, runs away with you. Any girl who acts like you do should be prepared to take her punishment. And what that will be if you go on the way you are is anybody's guess. I might heed Cleopatra's words and rectify the omissions of your childhood and take you over my knee, or I might take you up on what you're offering."

"You're not human at all; you're a beast," she spat at him in fury.

Their eyes locked for a long, frozen moment; perhaps his composure wasn't as secure as she had believed, because he seemed to be restraining himself from committing physical violence.

"Just watch it, you silly little fool. You don't know what you're talking about or how lucky you are that I'm the one you picked to take for a ride. You could have come up against a real monster, someone who'd resort to brute mayhem to get his pound of flesh. You could have landed yourself in deep trouble. Some men make mean lovers and ask things of a woman you don't know anything about, and I hope to God you never do. What I came to say is this: Even though you've welched on me, it's still to my advantage to make the best of a bad bargain. In fact, thinking about it, this way suits me better."

"Paul, perhaps I'm as stupid as you say I am. I haven't understood a word you've said."

"How much more clearly do I have to spell it out? I need the cover more than I need the woman. The

pretense that we're on . . . close terms will do. You put
up a good performance tonight. Keep it up and that will
square the books.''

"Paul, I'm sorry. Please don't be angry with me—but
I don't know what you're saying. Oh, I know that you
want the others to think that we're lovers, but I don't
know why."

"You can't have missed the gossip," he ground out in
bitterness. "The vultures of the press had a field day."

"What gossip?" she asked weakly, knowing that she
was making him angrier still, but refusing to pretend
that she knew what he was getting at when she didn't.

"What are you trying to do to me, Catherine?"

"I'm not trying to do anything, except understand."

"All right. But if you're being funny, expect to be
paid back. The gossip concerning Zoe and Jeremy."

"Oh *that*."

"Yes, *that*. The other story, the one not in the
screenplay, caused more talk and trauma and human
pathos and drama than anything in the script. It
certainly made quite a rumpus when Zoe fell in love
with her co-star under the direction of her boyfriend."

Catherine wondered why Paul was bringing this up
now; it was hardly relevant to them. She also wondered
at the bitterness on his face. Had he been a special
friend of the director who had been given such a bad
deal? Or was it something more? Had he fallen for Zoe
himself?

"I've never seen such feeling on a set. The critics set
Zoe up on a pedestal for her fireball performance. They
called her brilliant . . . the most exciting discovery of
the decade . . . a sensational mixture of whore and
angel, harlot and innocent. She was referred to as the
actress destined to add even more bubbles to the
champagne scene. They said she acted everyone else
off the set and held their breath at the artless beauty of

the love scenes that reached a new dimension in film intimacy. Scorchingly intimate scenes played with art- less candor and innocence. They made film history. Hardened old cynics, stringent critics who'd seen it all before in a variety of guises, wept openly. At the other end of the scale, even the most straight-laced member of the public could view it without embarrassment. So there you are."

Even though she didn't understand this heart-to- heart, or what message it was supposed to convey, it brought a gigantic, equally inexplicable lump to her throat.

"Women!" He spat out the word in vengeance. "They're not worth bothering about. What's so special about Zoe? All women are brilliant actresses. They don't care about a man, except in terms of what he can do for them, whether it's giving them a good time or promoting their careers. Women are born with the intuitive knowledge of how to get the most, and give the smallest possible return. Isn't that so, Catherine?"

Even if everything he'd said was still a mystery to her, she could now identify the lump in her throat. It was compassion for his jaundiced opinion of her sex.

"I feel sorry for you, Paul. It must be horrible to have such a warped mind."

"And who warped it? Have you asked yourself that?"

Her pity proved to be the final straw, the one that forced him to step forward and take her by the arms. She stiffened in dread of the shaking she expected to receive. But instead she found herself being propelled smoothly forward and kissed violently. She hadn't been lying when she said she felt sorry for him. He had been driven to this by his own bitterness; because she felt sympathy for him she didn't repulse him, even found it in her heart to rejoice that she was helping him to get it out of his system. Being kissed in anger was a totally new experience for her. Not only her mouth suffered the outrage; it was as though her emotions were being peeled raw by the savagery of his passion. She clung to him, supine beneath the malevolent force of his desire, throwing her neck back to give her mouth up to his kiss.

She should have known it wouldn't stop there, at the baring of her emotions. She was divested of her clothes in such a way that she hardly noticed what was happening. Here was no impatient boy out for his own gratification with no thought for her. She was in the hands of an expert who knew the value of a pause, a caress, a man experienced enough to draw her from quiescence and make her aware of her own needs before attempting to satisfy his own.

His fingers grazed down the strained column of her throat, and down again to the rounded temptation of her bared breast. She reveled in the sensuous, sensual feeling, the mindless ecstasy of the abrasive backward and forward movement that was both unbearable torment and impossible delight. She knew she should do something to stop him—now, before it was too late—but she couldn't summon up the willpower to speak out against the things he was doing. To have him desist now would be torment beyond imagining.

His mouth lifted from hers, but only to find a more vulnerable target to plunder. It teased down her throat, following the exact course his fingers had taken, and parted to enclose the rosy tip of her breast, sending shock-waves of pure unadulterated joy tingling through her system that were incomparable to anything she had ever known before. Another first, because it was the first time a man's lips had ever become acquainted with such an intimate part of her body. She had thought kissing was only for mouths. The exhilarating surprise to a body that was unprepared for such delights was too traumatic to take and she began to shiver uncontrollably. Yet even though she pushed him away, it wasn't in her mind to reject him. She was overwhelmingly certain that he knew this, knew she needed a second or so to get herself together, and she couldn't believe it when he made no attempt to take her back into his arms.

Her eyes flew up to his for explanation.

"I've got to live with myself afterward," he grunted. With typical male brusqueness and lack of feeling, he added, "I should have waited until morning. This is no time to talk."

"Why are you so contradictory?" she demanded furiously. "You came in here saying you wanted to talk; now you say it's no time to talk. It's about time you decided on something and kept to it. You never wanted me here in the first place. It was in your eyes when you met me at the airport, yet *you* hired me and *you* sent my air ticket to me. I didn't invite you into my room just now. You pushed your way in. And it might also pay you to remember that I didn't undress myself. You did that. You wanted to make love to me. Are you telling me now that you don't?"

"Cool it, will you?"

"Cool it!" she exploded. "How dare you? I've made a discovery." He'd accused her often enough of having a provocative tongue; she might as well give it some exercise. "I thought this was something that only applied to women. But you've shown me there's such a thing as a *male* tease."

Retribution beat down upon her head for goading him when she saw the intensity of his reaction. She thought he was going to blow a fuse as he lashed back in retaliation. "All right—you've asked for this. It's that old devil double standard raising its chauvinistic head again. I like the women I make love to to at least make a pretense of clinging to their ideals. Putting it on a commercial basis cheapens it. It's one thing for a man to show his appreciation for a woman's favors, but the price tag should be discreetly tucked out of sight, not flaunted in advance."

She didn't understand this any more than she'd understood the other strange things he'd said, but she recognized an insult when it was thrown at her. "Get out. Get out before I—" Looking 'round wildly for something to hit him with, her eyes fastened on the book he'd returned. The fact that he'd written it gave the act of hurling it at him a flavor of poetic justice.

He caught it, of course. She hadn't expected him to be a sitting duck. Neither had she expected what followed.

"Thanks," he said, an insufferable smirk coming to his face. "I haven't read this one, although I've read most of the other stuff he's churned out. Don't suppose I'll get much sleep after this, so I might as well see how old Lucian makes out in his latest offering."

"You haven't read—? *He?* Who are you talking about?"

"Lucian Chance. Writes, of course, under the pseudonym Lucky Chance. He was at the party where we first met. Tall, owlish, self-effacing type. Doesn't have a great deal to say for himself. You wouldn't think that words were his stock in trade."

Chapter Nine

She let him go without asking any more questions or offering an explanation as to why she collapsed, thunder-struck, upon the bed. For one thing, she didn't have a voice at her disposal; she was barely capable of registering a grunt of disbelief as he strode out the door leading to the balcony to return to his own room. Secondly, her thoughts were in too much of a bewildered spin for her to have known what to ask.

Paul wasn't Lucky Chance. Lucky Chance, real name Lucian Chance, was the tall, pale-faced man wearing brown spectacles whom she'd seen at the party, the one who'd looked so nice, modest and naturally retiring that she had dismissed him as too ordinary to be a writer. She had looked 'round for someone extraordinary and had latched on to the wrong man. How could she have made such a ghastly mistake?

Who was Paul? Paul Hebden, that's who he was. She didn't have to search far to discover what he did for a living. To her painful cost, she knew. It all clicked together. Every word, every action, all the puzzling, mystifying things, suddenly gained crystal clarity. Paul's reference to the gossip circulating about Zoe, Jeremy—and Paul himself, because Paul was the film director who'd been cuckolded. . . . His need to save face and his obsessive desire to show her off like some prize trophy . . . The bored arrogance and ill-

concealed contempt toward Poppy and that other clinging female at Lois's party, as well as toward any
other—and there would have been many—foolish girl
who made it clear that her body was available to him in
exchange for a leg up the ladder of success in the film
industry . . . All explained.

She remembered how, earlier that day, she and
Deirdre had speculated on the absence of the film
director and his live-in girl friend. But they hadn't been
absent at all. They'd been there all the time. Paul was
the director, which made her—she swallowed in alarm
—his live-in girl friend.

She could kick herself for not digging deeper. At
Lois's party she had known that Paul was making a pass
at her, but she had still persisted in offering her services
to him. Good, old-fashioned, respectable secretarial
services. But he'd assumed something else, as of course
he would have, since he wasn't a writer and had no use
for an efficient typist. He had thought she was engaged
in a profession that dated much farther back, one that
was on the go before the typewriter had been invented,
as far back as biblical times, the oldest profession in the
world. He thought . . . painful as this was to her she
had to take it to its bitter conclusion . . . that he had
bought the right to share her bed. He thought he had
hired her as his mistress.

Even as her cheeks flamed, she could understand
Paul's part in this, why he'd brought her. A tag-along
female would nip further speculation in the bud. If he
had a new woman in his bed, no one was going to think
he was still pining for the one who'd jumped out of it,
and he could direct his ex and her new lover through all
the steamy love scenes without everyone's thinking he
was going through every kind of torment.

She certainly had the knack of landing herself in the
most bizarre situations; this one topped the lot. She

could see how it had come about. She had gone to the
party for the specific purpose of meeting Lois's author
friend, with a preconceived notion of what the writer of
racy, action-packed detective novels would look like.
Never again would she be stupid enough, impulsive
enough, to prejudge anything or anybody. It was, she
realized, gravely winding a strand of hair 'round her
finger and giving it a hard tug, as if seeking solace in
self-punishment, to Paul's credit that he hadn't wanted
her to be brazen enough to carry it through. That's why
he'd given her time to back out, had seemed to be
pressing that option on her, and why he'd been so
disapproving when he met her at the airport—and why
he thought he had an absolute right to be on familiar
terms with her. She glowed all over with shame as she
recalled the mockery and contempt in his eyes all the
times when she had drawn back from his touch and how
he had accused her of welching on a deal. A deal she
had so unwittingly and innocently made. And her
embarrassment increased a hundredfold when she remembered her most recent humiliation. She hadn't
drawn back just now, but he had. Even he had balked
at having sex with a whore.

But I'm not! A protesting tear slid down her cheek to
be impatiently scrubbed away. You're not a child,
either, she scolded herself. Two more truths flashed
into her mind. She wasn't a welcher. And she wasn't
going to get one wink of sleep until she'd seen Paul and
made that point clear to him.

She reached for her robe, but her hand was curiously
hesitant. It was old and tatty, one of the few items of
clothing she hadn't purchased especially for this trip. It
seemed to represent youth and innocence, and she felt
that in view of everything it would be hypocritical to
put it on. Furthermore, she didn't want to present an
appearance that might play on his sympathy. She

selected, instead, a caftan from her wardrobe and
pulled it over her head. It was another of the things
Ally had persuaded her to buy, saying it would be
marvelous for casual evening wear, or to double glam-
orously as a robe. At the time Catherine had been
unable to envision an occasion when she might want to
wear it. It was very beautiful and exotic in parchment-
colored silk, with a trail of vivid flowers in glowing
orange and gold shades sweeping down from her
breasts to the floor-length hem. Yes, this would serve
her purpose better. Her purpose? No . . . no, not that.
She just wanted to explain to Paul that she wasn't what
he thought she was.

Cleopatra had laid out her hairbrush set. She picked
up the ivory-backed brush and restored order to her
hair, which hung past her shoulder blades. Its weight
and lustrous dark copper sheen were well suited to its
simple style, but Catherine wondered whether the time
had come to try a more sophisticated hair-do. Not
at this moment, though; she was in too much of a
hurry. She had to get it over quickly before her courage failed her. After hurriedly examining her face to
ensure that it wasn't tear-stained, and ignoring the
acute misery in her enormous sapphire-blue eyes,
she left her room to run along the balcony to his
door.

He answered her tap instantly, almost as if he had
been waiting for her to come, then bade her enter, his
face solemn and guarded.

"I have to talk to you," she said, not realizing that
they were the same words he'd used earlier when he
had come to her room under pretext of returning her
book, until he queried, "Talk?" with the same eloquent
lift of his brows that she had employed.

"I didn't really expect you to make it easy for me,"
she said. In a hushed voice that exactly matched her

lowered chin, she added, "I've come to tell you that I'm not a welcher."

"You've come to pay up?"

That wasn't it at all. She'd come to explain. But something in his face goaded her to say, "If you insist, yes."

"I can't hear you. Speak up," he commanded.

Her heart was fluttering against her ribs and she knew she sounded breathless, but this time she managed a louder voice. "I said yes."

"You're quite sure about that?" The fixed penetration of his gaze caused her to color. It wasn't the only giveaway thing she did, but the other wasn't made clear to her until he disentangled her fingers from her hair. "I think we'd better sit down, in a reasonable adult manner, and figure this out."

She didn't realize what he meant by "reasonable adult manner" until he sat down on the edge of the bed, legs apart in typical male fashion, and gave her a perch on one of them.

"There, isn't that better? Cozier, wouldn't you say?" he inquired, his hand stealing under her hair.

"Yes," she said, falling back on that faint little voice again, striving to dispel her painful awareness of his thumb sensually stroking the nape of her neck.

"So you want to begin fulfilling your duties, do you?"

"If that's what you want."

"I didn't catch that. What did you say?"

"I said yes."

"Right—into bed with you. Well?" he snapped when she didn't jump into action. "What are you waiting for?"

"N–nothing," she said miserably, and dutifully attempted to slide off his knee.

His hand dropped with the swiftness of a bullet from

her neck to trap its intended target, her waist, preventing her from moving. His free hand tilted her chin and made it impossible for her not to look directly at him.

"You haven't got the monopoly on deep thinking, you know. My thoughts have been working overtime since I left you."

"Oh?" The realization that he had been teasing her forced an even deeper color into her cheeks, then drained it out again.

"How many times has a man undressed you before tonight?"

"I wasn't counting."

"You wouldn't have been old enough to count, that's why. And the man who did the chore would have been your father."

"Aren't you the bright boy!" she said, resorting to flippancy.

"No, I've been extremely dull. I should have wised up much sooner than I did. All the signs were there even before that ridiculous scene in your room just now. I want you to know that what I did to you isn't generally considered outrageous."

"I wasn't outraged."

"You were petrified. When I . . . well . . . I know it was a shock to you, but it was a shock to me when you seemed all set to shoot through the ceiling as though you'd been scalded. You were trembling so much I thought you were going to pass out on me. I couldn't quite make up my mind whether it was another of your tricks to fend me off, or if it was for real. The suspicion *had* gone through my mind that you just might possibly be a virgin in the accepted sense, that you'd never consummated a relationship with a man. But I never for a moment dreamed that it was *all* virgin territory. I'm not embarrassing you, am I, by speaking this frankly?"

"Oh *no!* It's . . . er . . . fascinating. Do go on."

"Poor little kitten. You can hardly bear to look at me. Why didn't you stop me? I don't mean the talking about it, but the doing. All you had to say was that no man had got that far with you before, and we both would have been spared that fiasco."

She swallowed, feeling bitterly hurt. She hadn't been able to help the upheaval of her emotions when his lips had touched her breast. True, the effect of it had almost rocketed her into orbit, but she had looked upon it as a blissful awakening. How could he bring it down to such a debasing level by calling it a fiasco?

"I apologize for what I put you through. I would never have subjected you to my . . . unseemly behavior . . . if I'd known."

Unseemly behavior! It was getting worse. Turning a lovely moment into something tainted and shabby.

"I should have recognized that you weren't being provocative," he continued remorselessly. "I should have known that that innocent look was genuine. Do you remember when you told me you were called Cat for short and I said something about it being a sinfully inaccurate description, and that I had a much more appropriate pet name in mind? I didn't realize how right I was. You *are* a kitten-face . . . a tiny misunderstood kitten who doesn't possess enough sense to come in out of the rain." He laughed harshly. "We've been at cross-purposes from the beginning. Your answers were totally different from the ones I usually get when I chat a girl up. I accused you of talking in riddles and presumed it must be a new kind of party talk."

"I thought you were telling me you didn't want to talk business," said Catherine.

"I don't know about talking about it; I know that I meant it. But I think not the same kind of business you meant. You'd better tell me what it's all about. Begin with Allycats. Tell me just what Allycats is, and we'll go from there."

"A typewriting agency. At the interview—"

"What interview?" he cut in.

"When I came to your hotel room."

"That was an interview? As far as I knew it was a date. I thought I was taking you out to dinner. If only I'd tested you out as you asked me to . . . or, should I say, tried to test you out, because somehow I don't think I'd have got very far. Either way, it would have saved us both a lot of aggravation."

"I was referring to a dictation and typing test, which seemed very reasonable. Dare I ask what you thought I meant?"

"I think you know."

"Yes. You thought I meant a quick tumble on the mattress," she said indignantly.

"Before you start letting off steam, I didn't take you up on it."

"I'm wondering why," she scoffed.

"I didn't hold you that cheap."

"I'll go along with that. The check you gave me would have made it quite an expensive little get-together. I thought the fee was high for shorthand and typing duties. Perhaps it's normal for the service you had in mind."

"Why are you insulting me?" he asked, his voice grating with anger. "I haven't insulted you. I have never paid for sex in my entire life. I couldn't believe my ears when you insisted on putting it on a commercial footing. I gave you every chance to have second thoughts. I didn't expect to see you at Nassau airport."

"I know," she admitted, sighing heavily. "It's all been a terrible mix-up. I was stunned when we had connecting rooms at the hotel in New Providence, with no apparent sign of a key."

"It might help if you told me just how you arrived at the crazy idea that I needed a shorthand typist."

"I thought you were someone else. I went to that party for the sole purpose of meeting Lucky Chance, because Lois, our hostess, said that he was on the lookout for someone to type his manuscripts. It was Lois who pointed him out to me. Of course, at the time he was talking to you. So numbskull here picked the wrong man. I jumped to the conclusion that you were the author and then, when you confirmed it, I—"

"Hold it right there. You've just lost me again. You said I confirmed it? By what mistaken notion did you latch on to that?"

"I asked you if I should call you Lucky."

"I don't believe it!" he groaned. "If my memory serves me correctly, I said, 'You tell me.' I was hoping I'd be lucky."

"I guess, party atmosphere or no party atmosphere, I should have stuck to formality and addressed you as Mr. Chance."

"It would have straightened me out. I know I quite fancied you, but you'd been giving pretty heavy stand-off signs and I didn't know whether or not I'd be lucky enough to make it with you."

"*Make it* with me! Did you really think you'd get me into bed as quickly as that? I find that disgusting!"

"It's no good talking like that. It won't help matters any. We've got to consider where we go from here."

"I know where *I* go from here—home. I don't know how long it will take me, but I promise to pay you back in full."

"You don't owe me a thing. The money's not important. I accept now that you didn't deliberately set out to fleece me."

"It might not be important to you, but it is to me. It's a matter of honor for me to pay you back, and the sooner I get home and start earning, the sooner that can be achieved."

"Catherine, this is difficult enough as it is, so will you let me finish saying what I have to say without interruptions? That is not a request, it's an order. Is that understood?"

"Perfectly. It may have been unknowing on my part, but I entered into a contract. I sold my body to you. I am yours to command. Whatever you desire of me, I must do."

"If you aren't the most infuriating female I've ever known . . . If you don't button up for five minutes, I just might exercise my rights in accordance with the terms of the contract as I thought them to be, instead of offering to negotiate fresh ones. Are you prepared to listen, damn you?"

"Yes!" she snapped belligerently.

"When you propositioned me—as I thought," he was quick to add when her mouth opened as if she was going to protest, "it came like a gift straight from heaven. Normally I would have sent you off with a flea in your ear, because I like to do the propositioning. But your timing was fantastic. I was all set to come out here, not particularly looking forward to stirring up all the old gossip, when you dropped the perfect solution into my hands. Bringing you here would scotch it before it even started. You're with me? You know what I'm talking about?"

"Mmmm. Coral Cay was the location for *Edge of Paradise*. A sequel is about to be made. You're here in connection with that."

"Carry on, you're doing just fine," he encouraged.

"I thought, while I was still laboring under the misapprehension that you were an author, that you were here to do the screenplay. It's obvious that you're a very important member of the film crew, so you must be the director. The one who—" She held tightly to her intrepid tongue.

"You can finish it without fear of reprisal. You don't have to spare my feelings; after all, nobody else does. Or, if you're too squeamish, I'll do it for you. I'm the sucker who directed his girl into the arms of another guy."

"I'm sorry. Zoe is very beautiful and it must have been particularly distressing for you to have to sit back and watch them falling more deeply in love every day."

"Putting the lines in their mouths, even, creating a conducive atmosphere and demanding sizzling realism in the love scenes. You could say that it was not one of my better times," he admitted wryly. "So you see how intolerable my position would be if you suddenly packed up and went home."

"Now that you point it out to me, I do. So what are you suggesting?"

"That you stay and earn your fee. And before you start biting my head off again, I don't mean under the sheets. You gave quite a commendable performance this evening as the new woman in my life. There were times when you looked at me as though you really had taken a terrific tumble for me. I was most impressed. I want you to stay and keep up the pretense that we're having an affair. If you can bring yourself to tolerate my attentions in full view of an audience, you have my solemn word that I won't step out of line in private."

She blinked. Tolerate him? Didn't he know the effect he had on her? He had only to look at her to make her melt; at his touch her normally sane system went crazy. And, as if she didn't have enough to deal with, now that she understood the reason for his attitude to women, why he held her sex in scorn and contempt, even her dislike of the kind of man he typified no longer had any potency. No wonder he was like he was. Her heart ached to think what *Edge of Paradise* had cost him. It must have taken him to the edge of hell to have to guide Zoe, the woman he loved, through all those torrid love scenes. The critics had raved about her talented performance, but he had known that her brilliance in the role owed everything to realism, that every tender look and unbridled burst of passion was a genuine portrayal of her true feelings for her co-star. On top of that, he'd had to endure the knowledge that he was both an object of pity and the laughingstock of the entire unit. No wonder he wanted her to stay. He wouldn't want to subject himself to the mockery of the cast and crew for a second time by having another girl walk out on him.

There was no question of her leaving him in the lurch. She had to support the belief that she was his woman. But what would that do to her, knowing that he only wanted her to remain because of her usefulness, not because he felt anything for her? What he asked her to do in public would be easy. The difficulties would arise when they were alone and she had to feign indifference. Feeling as vibrantly aware of him as she did, with no drama school training behind her to fall back on, how was she going to pull that one off? Where was her support to come from? The answer to that popped unbidden into her mind. She still had her pride. That would keep her from revealing how she felt about him.

"What do you say, Catherine? It will mean putting on a bit of a show when the others are present, but I'll try not to do anything objectionable. I'm sure you won't find it too onerous to play up to me, put on an act that you care."

She could confidently guarantee the performance of a lifetime. It wouldn't even be acting.

"I'll give it a try," she said.

"Thank you. I could have handled it, but the situation might have been somewhat uncomfortable if your decision had gone the other way."

"Would you have accepted the alternative answer?" she asked, just a little wearily.

"I think not," he replied, back in top arrogant form. "You won't lose out. In private, I'll treat you like a kid sister. But at the end there'll be a bonus for you. A trinket, the kind of appreciative thank you a brother would never give to his little sister."

"I'll get a good holiday out of this. Give your appreciative thank-you gift to someone who's earned it. I don't want a trinket for services I haven't rendered," she said savagely.

Some members of the film crew began to arrive the next day. Within three days the full team was in residence, not in Gus's house, but in the makeshift village that was set up a gentle ten minutes stroll away. Gus's spacious home was taken over and made into a mini studio with rooms renamed production office, wardrobe, make-up, props department and so on. Wide new roads, made to accommodate the bulky impedimenta of filming during the shooting of *Edge,* were recleared and, in some instances, fresh ones made, with due care taken to preserve the nature-run-riot setting necessary for *Return to Paradise.*

Now that work had commenced, Catherine was conscious of an electric change in the atmosphere. Her fears of how she would carry off her deception of being indifferent to Paul when she was alone with him proved to be groundless. As the days passed they were hardly ever alone. He was the generator on which the others charged themselves up. He rose before everyone else and went to bed later, every second packed to capacity, and if he could have stretched the day to fit in more work, Catherine felt that he would have done so. Not knowing anything about the exorbitant daily running costs of making a film and the tightness of the budget he was operating on, she felt that he was driving himself too hard and heading, by deliberate intent, for a nervous breakdown.

But when she expressed this fear to Cleopatra, the genial face broke into its customary white-toothed smile. "Bless you, no, Miss Catherine. It's always the same when filming starts. Work, work, work. No time for fun, only snapping tempers. Always the feeling that it's never going to come right. But it always does."

As Catherine hadn't yet managed to be up in time to share breakfast with him, the only occasions she managed to share with Paul were lunchtimes and the evening meal. The latter they took at Gus Strindberg's table, alongside Zoe and Jeremy. Sometimes another member of the cast or crew would be invited to join them; always the talk concerned some aspect of the day's shooting which Catherine knew nothing about, and so she was precluded from taking part in the conversation. But Paul occasionally picked up her hand and kept it for a while—and she didn't mind one tiny bit having to eat her food with only the use of one hand. Or he'd send her a smile of sweet intimacy that would turn her stomach over, even though she knew it was a bond specially created for the benefit of the others.

The constraint she had sensed between Zoe and Jeremy was now no longer a suspicion in her mind but a cast-iron certainty. Their boredom with one another was embarrassingly obvious; if they hadn't already made the break, the rift was certainly getting wider every day. It was Catherine's firm belief that they were now lovers on the set only.

In one of her many idle moments she had managed to get hold of a copy of the shooting script, and read it with mounting excitement. *Edge of Paradise* had been acclaimed as exceptional, but *Return* had a few interesting twists of its own and promised to excel a film that, they had said, couldn't be bettered. *Edge of Paradise* had ended with the hero and heroine doing the right thing and going back to their own partners. *Return* took up the story to show that their partners had not led celibate lives in their absences and their coming back brought its own crop of problems and frustrations, although the hero and heroine each assumed that the other had returned to marital bliss. Unknown to one another, they returned to the island they had lived on as castaways and there followed a reunion scene that was passionate and poignant, tender and tempestuous. Catherine wondered cynically if they were managing to inject the required amount of feeling and fervor into their lovemaking as demanded by the script. Acting was their business, so they could probably fake it. She knew that she would have found it repulsive to lie with someone and simulate feelings that had cooled.

She further wondered if Paul was aware that Zoe had lost interest in Jeremy, or that the dynamic brunette beauty was now using her wiles to get him back. Strictly speaking, Zoe's mouth was too thin to be called sensual, but she'd learned how to make the most of what she'd got and could pout to enchanting effect. And she pouted more often at Paul than discretion permitted. When Paul told her about a performance that hadn't been up to scratch, she had a way of pushing out her lower lip a fraction and achieving a tiny tremble that matched the hurt and the heartrending plea for leniency in the liquid dark depths of her oloroso-colored eyes. If Paul was affected by this he kept it under guard, but it was noticeable that he never lost his temper with her. With amazing patience he would painstakingly go over a point he thought she might have missed. But then again, neither did he show any outward sign of antagonism toward Jeremy. It seemed as though he had cast all personal issues aside. Nothing in Paul's manner showed that the leading man had stolen Zoe from him, which, Catherine supposed, was a sign of his true professionalism.

In contrast to the elaborate evening meal, the lunchtime arrangements were casual and relaxed. Each member of the team collected a box lunch and ate it on the set. Catherine made herself responsible for Paul's lunch box. She checked the daily call sheet each morning to find out where filming was taking place that day, and then she'd set off to that part of the island.

If she arrived early, which she often did purposely, no one seemed to mind her taking the role of spectator. She was early on one particular day and settled down to watch. Even with her lack of knowledge, she recognized Paul's worth as a director; he seemed to see things quicker than anyone else, and he knew instinctively when to sharp-talk, bully or beguile to get a reaction. As if it was putty in his hands, he molded each scene to his exact liking. Sometimes he'd ask an actor to step aside and he would say the lines as he wanted them said. It was funny and, predictably, attracted cracks from the camera crew when he took Zoe's place in a love scene with Jeremy to show her how he wanted it done. But it wasn't so funny, for Catherine, anyway, when Jeremy was the one he asked to step aside.

"No, Jeremy, not like that. Move over a second and I'll show you."

Why, oh why, had she had to get there early to see this? Catherine asked herself wretchedly as Paul took Zoe into his arms. It didn't help to see the bright gleam of triumph in Zoe's eyes that told her the clever star had deliberately maneuvered it. She had been stiff and unresponsive with Jeremy so that Paul would have to take her into his arms to demonstrate how to coax the required reaction from her.

An unnatural hush settled over the set; even the many brightly colored little birds in the trees stopped their incessant twittering as Paul and Zoe went through the preliminary facial expressions, then touched. Paul's features were expressive of the agony of a man savoring a moment long hungered for. His hands skimmed down from Zoe's shoulders to trap her hands, possessive, yet deferential. Then he opened Zoe's arms wide and drew them 'round his own waist, before gently drawing her fully into his arms. The build up of tension was terrific. Yet when he began to kiss her it was as if everything that had gone before had been completely low key.

It was so devouring and real that Catherine couldn't bear to watch and she realized even more acutely how Paul must have felt during the earlier shooting, when he had known that he was losing Zoe to Jeremy. Did Paul know what was common knowledge to everyone else, that Zoe was making a deliberate play for him? Would he take her back?

The kiss ended, the birds started chirruping again, the team launched into natural activity and everything clicked back to normal as Paul straightened up, looking as coolly unruffled as if that turbulent demonstration hadn't taken place.

"Something along those lines, Jeremy," he said.

The rehearsal went satisfactorily enough for Paul to call a lunch break for the rest of them while the cameras were being set up. Observing their usual routine, Catherine and Paul wandered farther down the beach where the scene was to be shot, away from the others. She was hungry, but as she unpacked the box that contained food for two, she felt too emotional to eat. The sun was hot on her face and bare shoulders, but there was a cold hollow feeling in her stomach and her thoughts were in turmoil. A dove cooed loudly in the branches of a sea grape tree. Her eyes took in the beauty of coconut palms, swaying casuarinas, sugar apple trees and more exotic flowers than were within her power to name. So much peace all around her, so much chaos within.

Her jealousy was without cause, she told herself. Theirs was a convenient arrangement; Paul had made no commitment to her.

"You did very well just now," Paul said, having observed, along with the rest of the people who had been there, her smoldering reaction to his scene with Zoe. He was stretched out on his back in a pose of utter relaxation. He bit deep into a sandwich and chewed it thoughtfully before adding, "That jealous look was very convincing."

The words were light; it was the warm way he was appraising her from lazy eyes that sent ripples of feeling through her body and made her want to slide down by his side.

"You shouldn't eat while lying down," she said. "I'm sure it's not a good thing to do."

Those lazy eyes, brilliant beneath their frond of sunbleached lashes, flicked over her, kindly scathing in their criticism as his lips delivered a rebuke. "Don't overdo it, kitten-face. I don't allow women to tell me what is or isn't good for me."

"Sorry! Choke on the crumbs for all I care!"

She tried to look away. Her nerves were like crossed wires and she was paying scant attention to her own lunch. But she couldn't seem to drag her eyes away from him. The term good-looking was too all-encompassing to do him justice and was light-years away from the truth. He was magnificent. The proud, majestic head; the long, lean torso clad in a figure-molding sweat shirt; the long, athletic legs in sand-colored jeans. This Paul was a long way removed from the immaculate man who came to the dinner table each evening; he was somehow far more disturbing. The fierce midday sun shimmering through the treetops with a lacy amber opalescence brightened his hair to pirate gold. The direction her thoughts were taking, as well as keying her up to a heady pitch of excitement, was most appropriate. There was a certain something about his appearance in casual garb that made him look—what was the word she was searching for? Swashbuckling! Since coming to Coral Cay he'd grown a beard. How it suited him, even if it did heighten his already considerable male virility and make him look more devil-may-care arrogant than before! Buccaneerish—this Paul would have been at home sailing the seas in the days when the Caribbean had been called The Spanish Main, right down to the cut on his right cheek which he'd acquired somewhere and which looked as though it needed a dab of antiseptic. But she wasn't going to tell him and get another scolding for concerning herself about him. Why, when a woman's feelings for a man deepened, did it suddenly become an obsession with her to fuss over him?

When Paul went back to work she made no attempt to accompany him, preferring the company of her own disquieting thoughts to running the risk of seeing Zoe in his arms again. They were poisonous thoughts, the serpent in this paradisical place, this corner of Eden.

She tried to push them out by filling her mind and senses with the beauty around her. The heavily scented frangipani, wild orchids, ginger flowers, bougainvillea, oleanders, jasmine, and numerous trees and vines, all combined to form a tangled semicircle of leaf, flower and shrub which edged the dazzling spectacle of white coral sand. Beyond, crystal water deepened into a lagoon of such a brilliant blue that it defied credibility.

She should have been in heaven. Nothing more arduous was asked of her than to be nice in public to an extremely personable man. Not any man. One super-special, supercharged, exceptional man. Why couldn't she accept her amazing piece of luck and enjoy it to the full?

If only she had some inbuilt protection to hide behind, but no man was an island, and that was even more true when applied to woman—to her. She would never be entire of herself, or inviolate, where Paul was concerned. She would never be able to shut him out of her thoughts . . . or her heart. Why had she had to spoil everything by falling in love with him?

Perhaps this was the biggest revelation of all. How had it happened? And when? The attraction she had felt for him had slid so gently into love that she hadn't known it was happening until it was an established fact. Yet, looking back, she ought to have known. The strong stirrings of physical attraction might have made it easy for him to get close to her, but it couldn't have seemed so right, her thoughts wouldn't have been so tender toward him, her jealousy of Zoe so acute, if her heart hadn't been affected.

She should have picked up the clues and armored herself against the stupidity of falling in love with someone who was inaccessible to her. Someone whose heart hankered after another woman.

Chapter Ten

Her tender feelings for Paul gave her the insight to know that he still loved Zoe. At the moment he was holding himself aloof from her, but how long would he allow his pride to stand in the way of what he wanted?

Perhaps pride wasn't the only consideration. It could be that he was too conscientious to take time off to sort out the tangles of his private life. Perhaps he intended to wrap up the film before dealing with personal issues.

She was a novice where filming was concerned, but even she knew that things weren't going as well as they should be and required Paul's total concentration. Not only was Zoe living up to the reputation that superstars had for being temperamental, but, in Catherine's opinion, she overstepped all bounds. She was difficult and impossibly rude to the other members of the cast and crew, with the exception of Paul. She saved all her smiles for him. As far as Zoe's pride was concerned, she didn't seem to have any in connection with Paul. It was sickening the way she drooled over him and found ways of getting close to him.

She walked off the set one day while Catherine was watching, leaving poor Jeremy fuming, to go up to Paul. Her stance was that of a docile little girl, but there was nothing little girlish about the face that stared up at him from beneath its curtain of silky dark hair. It was a woman's face, as warm and inviting as the sensuous undertones in her voice as she said, "I know I'm getting it wrong, Paul. I'm so stupid, darling. And so undeserving of your patience with me."

"Maybe it isn't all your fault, Zoe. This scene doesn't feel right, somehow. Let's see if anything can be worked out."

Catherine wondered why it was always a love scene that had to be worked out.

"Don't forget what I'm always telling you, Zoe," Paul said. "You're not just making up to one man. Your aim is to seduce the entire male audience."

He could think what he liked. Zoe's aim was to seduce one man, and that was Paul. Catherine could hardly bear to watch as he gentled Zoe into playing the scene as he saw it in his mind.

"We'll have your face in close-up. The body shots can be slotted in later. The focus will be on your lips and eyes. Give the camera crew a bad time. When you see the sweat beading on their hot, agitated brows, you'll know you've got it right."

"He's good at arousing a woman's passions," Jeremy observed, a touch of bitterness in his voice.

Catherine's head twisted 'round. She hadn't realized that Jeremy had come up behind her until he spoke.

"Of course, who's in a position to know that better than you?"

"Who indeed!" she said carelessly.

"Doesn't it bother you to watch them?"

Not sure whether he was needling her or giving voice to his own feelings, Catherine studied his face. The latter, she decided. Poor Jeremy. He'd had his moment of triumph over the making of *Edge of Paradise,* but the shoe was on the other foot now, and he didn't like it one tiny bit.

"Paul is only doing his job."

A rasping laugh came from Jeremy's throat. "And

very nicely and effectively. Zoe certainly responds to him." He brought his eyes away to look Catherine full in the face. "Guess the boys behind the cameras aren't by themselves in having a bad time, but they have no one to sate their aroused passions on, poor devils. I don't think it will be much good your pleading a headache tonight."

"I never get headaches," Catherine said, meeting his eyes squarely.

"Lucky for some!"

"It won't be lucky for you if you don't get back on the set," Paul said, catching Jeremy's last comment as he strode toward them.

"You don't have to yell. I just thought Catherine might like some company. To stop her from feeling neglected."

"Thanks for your concern, even if it is unappreciated and totally unnecessary. Catherine knows exactly where she stands with me."

At least that was the truth, Catherine thought as Jeremy walked away.

Instead of following him, as she expected, Paul hesitated for a moment. "He wasn't being fresh with you, was he?"

"No."

"Good." Paul bent down and touched his lips against her, lifted them briefly, and then came back again with more warmth, stirring sensations in her stomach which made the back of her neck tingle, while her hands wanted to slide up 'round his neck. If his lips hadn't released hers when they did she would have given way to the impulse.

That kiss, combined with the jealous way he'd looked and sounded, lifted her in exultation. But her spirits dropped just as quickly with the realization that he was putting on a show for the others. She reminded herself miserably that he never missed an opportunity of keeping up the charade that they were lovers.

That evening, at dinner, he was particularly demonstrative. He didn't just look at her, his eyes seemed to scorch over her in a way that stopped her breath. When he asked her if she'd care to take a stroll, she agreed readily. There was an element of tension 'round the table she was glad to get away from. Zoe and Jeremy showed all the signs of having had one ding-dong of a row, and Gus had been going on about rising costs attached to filming.

Paul and she walked hand in hand away from the house and out of sight of it, then stopped of one accord.

His fingers tilted her chin. "You're very lovely. You know that promise I was crazy enough to make to you, that in private I'd treat you like a kid sister?"

"Mm."

"Well, I think it's only fair to warn you that I'm finding it difficult to keep."

Without another word, his mouth came down on hers. Simultaneously her hands swept up 'round his neck and her fingers dug gloriously into the thickness of his hair.

She remembered Jeremy's wry words about her not being allowed to plead a headache. She knew that Paul had become steamed up while simulating that screen love scene with Zoe and he had to work it out of his system with someone. To her shame, she didn't care. She was even glad that it was her.

In the morning she might despise herself for her lack of pride, but tonight she had a hunger for him that was as fierce as his need of a woman. He had awakened feelings, given her an awareness of her own body, such as she had never known before.

Her lips parted in ecstasy as the kiss deepened; she was a responsive flame in his arms, pressing herself against him, molding herself to him in wanton, uncaring, fervent invitation. Her dress was low cut enough to give his hand free access. His fingers stole beneath her bra, easing the filmy covering of lace down below her fullness in an intimate foray that found the rosy tip which had once tingled in delight under his lips. She groaned, expressing her pleasure.

His voice was husky against her ear. "Shall we go back to the house?"

She knew he meant up to her room and not back to join the others. A tremor of expectation ran through her as she said, "Yes."

His mouth claimed hers in a kiss of fierce promise and they went back. But at her door he made no attempt to come in with her. She looked at him in question, and he said, "The old leopard never changes his spots. I gave you time to have second thoughts once before. I'm doing it again. I want you to be very sure, Catherine. Give yourself a moment to think, and if you're still of the same mind, my door will be open."

He continued on to his room, and she entered hers, closing the door behind her.

It was one thing to be carried along on the emotion of the moment, another to make the decision consciously. It didn't take Catherine very long to realize that she couldn't go through with something she knew was wrong. If Paul had had the right feelings for her it would have been different, but she could not let herself be used. On the other hand, she didn't like the thought of his waiting for her to come, and she knew that she wouldn't get much sleep herself if she didn't go and tell him. She was still fully dressed, so she didn't think he would get the wrong idea.

Before her courage failed her, she walked along their shared balcony, opened his door and entered his room, halting in her tracks when she saw that he wasn't alone.

"I'm sorry," she said, her heart dropping at the sight of Zoe.

"That's all right, Catherine. Zoe has a problem. There's something in tomorrow's script which she's not happy with."

"I'll leave you to sort it out, then," she said with feigned indifference.

"If you would." Paul came swiftly over to her, took her chin in his hand and kissed her firmly on the lips. "It won't take long, darling," he whispered urgently. "I promise."

"You don't have to promise a thing. Take as long as you like. All night if you want," she said, sweeping out the door, her chin held high.

She locked her balcony door, even though there was little chance of Paul's coming to it that night, in spite of what he'd said. He wouldn't need a substitute, not with Zoe there to finish what she'd started. Catherine undressed and got into bed, taking her fury out on the pillow, scrubbing her hand across her lips as if to erase the imprint of his.

She heard the outer door of Paul's room slam, and then soft footsteps padding along the balcony, followed by the distinctive noise of the handle of her balcony door being turned.

Then, "Open the door, Catherine," he commanded crisply. "It isn't what you think."

"No!" she called back. "It isn't what *you* think, either. I only came to tell you that I'd changed my mind. So go away."

When they met the next day, neither one of them made reference to the incident.

Tempers were reaching the flashpoint; there was enough friction on the set to cause a forest fire. Zoe accused Paul of being too critical with her and threatened to tear up her contract and go home. She upset everyone. The make-up girl wasn't speaking to her, the girl who gave the cues spoke only when absolutely necessary and Zoe's stand-in, a girl called Joanna, actually did walk out—or, to be more accurate, sailed out. She packed her bags and demanded to be taken off the island to the nearest airport, and even the fear of being sued for breach of contract wouldn't shift her from that decision.

Catherine wasn't certain what Joanna's duties as stand-in were, but she knew that her departure was causing Paul a lot of worry.

"I can't magic another girl up out of the air," he raged.

She knew that it wasn't so much having to rearrange the shooting schedule that was making him fume, such contingencies were the norm and he was well able to cope, but he couldn't justify the added costs due to lost shooting time if they had to hang about until another girl could be flown in.

Paul's answer to Gus's placatory, "Something will turn up," was a snort.

The three of them were sitting by the side of the pool. Filming had finished for the day. The two men were taking a pre-getting-ready-for-dinner drink. Catherine had just come out of the pool. She had gone in on impulse, having felt that the exercise would do her good and help her to work up an appetite, and she wasn't equipped with a towel. Rather than drip water all over the house, she had decided to wait until she'd dried off in the still-warm air before going up to her room.

In all innocence she asked, "Does Zoe need a stand-in? If this is the emergency you say it is, couldn't she stand in for herself?"

It seemed a reasonable thing to say, but Paul obviously thought otherwise. Beyond sending her a killing look, he didn't even bother to answer. Glass clinked heavily on glass as he slammed his almost-finished drink down on the glass-topped table before storming off.

"What's got into him?" she asked.

"Same as what's got into everyone," Gus replied. "Hard work in overpowering heat. Shut away in too small a community. Everyone expecting impossibilities of him, me included. A few days uninterrupted, tantrum-free shooting would have wrapped it up, and that's about all he's got . . . a few days, three at the most. The weather forecast isn't good. Waiting even half a day for another girl to arrive could prove fatal. Paul's got plenty to beef about."

"I know. It's been an eye-opener for me. I never realized that making a film was such hard work." Drawing her slim yet shapely legs up onto the lounger, hooking her fingers 'round her knees, she said, "I still don't see why Zoe should need a stand-in."

"Insurance," Gus replied tersely, meaning box-office insurance. Because who was going to pay to see a close-up of Zoe's less than beautiful body? Zoe owed her superb screen figure to subtle costume design and lost it the moment a scene called for her to take her clothes off, hence the need for a stand-in with perfect statistics.

Catherine thought he meant insurance against physical injury. She knew that big stars weren't allowed to take risks. For those who were prepared to do their own stunts the premiums were set artificially high, and so stand-ins were used more often than not. "I didn't realize there were any risky scenes in the film."

"There are several *very* risqué scenes," Gus said.

That was how the misunderstanding built up.

"Surely, in the circumstances, there's someone on the set who would fill in?" Catherine inquired.

Gus's eyes flicked impersonally over Catherine's excellent figure. "There is one girl who has the necessary requirements."

"Then why don't you ask her? Paul's very well respected. I don't think there's anyone here who wouldn't help him out of a fix if asked."

"You reckon?"

"I'm certain."

"Okay, I'm asking you."

"Me? But—I can't act."

"You don't need to. You trust Paul, don't you? He'll guide you through what you have to do. I should warn you, your name won't be on the credits. Your face will be shot from an obscure angle, or superimposed by Zoe's. But there will be a sizable fee in it for you."

"I'm not interested in the money or my name on the credits. I'll do it to help Paul, if you're sure I'll be good enough?"

Gus beamed at her. "Good enough? Joanna was selected from a whole bunch of hopefuls who were all eminently suitable, but if you'd been auditioning she wouldn't have stood a chance."

Catherine smiled. "You're just being kind."

She felt great, a modern-day Joan of Arc coming to the rescue. Yet later, up in her room, she was attacked by doubt. She couldn't see that she had done anything wrong in agreeing to fill in, but she felt uneasy. Paul would surely be pleased that she was willing to cooperate. He knew how guilty she felt when everyone else was working to peak capacity. She'd persuaded him to give her some routine office work to do and had taken on certain regular tasks, such as typing out the call sheets, the instructions given out each evening to all the cast and technicians to cover the next day's filming, but she still had too much free time on her hands. She wished she didn't have the queasy feeling that she ought to have talked it over with Paul before giving her word.

Paul's wrath broke over her that same evening. He barged into her room without knocking. She realized she ought to be grateful that she at least had clothes on. If he'd been five minutes earlier he would have caught her in the shower. As it was, she was extremely conscious of the brevity of her underwear and reached for her caftan, pulling it hurriedly over her head.

"Modesty?" he mocked. "After what Gus has just told me?"

"Presumably you mean about my taking Joanna's part as Zoe's stand-in?"

"I do."

"I don't know what you're getting into such a state about."

"Don't you?"

"I suppose you think it's presumptuous of me to think that I'm good enough. Gus said I'd be all right."

"Gus is right. I have a slight advantage over him and know that better than he does."

"Gus said I wouldn't have to do any acting and that you would guide me through the part."

"Fair enough. We'll have a run through now and see how you shape up. Any objections?"

"None."

"Then what are you waiting for?" he bellowed at her.

"For you to tell me what to do," she said, not without a touch of irritation of her own.

"You shouldn't need to be told what to do first. That much is obvious. Take off your clothes."

"My caftan?" she said, biting her lower lip as her fingers stole up to wind in her hair.

"Everything!"

"Paul . . . what are you saying?"

"How am I going to direct you if you're incapable of following such simple instructions. I said *everything.*"

"I . . . can't."

"You mean you'd prefer to wait until Jeremy and the camera boys are all there before you bare all? You confounded woman, didn't it penetrate that stupid skull of yours that you'd consented to do nude work?"

"No! I swear it didn't."

"What did you think?"

"Gus said something about insurance."

"Box-office insurance. Zoe is a talented actress and she has the kind of figure that dresses well, but without her clothes she's too skinny and loses her sex-symbol image."

"I didn't realize it was anything like that. I know that some scenes are considered too dangerous for the top stars to do, so stunt people are hired. I knew you wouldn't let me take too much of a risk, and so . . ." She gulped. "Can you get me out of it?" she asked miserably.

"It would serve you right if I said no. Put your mind at rest, you're out of it. And consider yourself lucky. I've had a blazing row with Gus for going behind my back to arrange it with you, and I've told him in no uncertain terms that I'm overruling your decision to accept."

"Thank you, Paul," she said meekly, realizing it was better than she deserved.

"In the future, be less impetuous and stop jumping to conclusions."

"There won't be a next time," she said emphatically.

"With your track record? I wouldn't take bets! Next time it will be something different; it always is. One of these days you're going to land yourself in deep trouble, and I might not be around to get you out."

"I'm sorry, Paul. Sorry to be a nuisance."

"Don't start the sob stuff," he warned. "That would really put the capper on it."

"I won't." She prayed he couldn't tell how difficult it was to keep the tears at bay.

"Come on," he said. "It's not the end of the world. Smile for me," he commanded.

But his kinder tone, after his anger, served to lower her chin further. His finger came out to tilt it, bringing it back up.

"What am I going to do with you, kitten-face?" It was a plea, a cry, a groan—and then she was brought into his arms and his mouth was hard and hungry on hers.

Just for a moment she tensed; then her fingers unclenched and her body relaxed, surrendering to the intoxicating power he had over her. For pride's sake she ought to put up some resistance; even a flimsy token stand would have salvaged some remnants of her self-respect. But she couldn't. She was both enslaved and excited by his virile masculinity. Her blood ran wild as his hands stroked up and down her back, burrowed under her hair to plunder the tender nape of her neck, then came over her shoulders and down to the tumultuous heaving of her breasts. His encircling fingers spread rings of joy throughout her entire system before sliding behind her to pinion her to him in a clamp of steel.

Her stomach muscles tightened and her breathing was rapid and shallow. With a pounding heart, her pulses jumping, she waited for him to divest her of her caftan and seek release. What she anticipated did not happen. Instead she recoiled in horrified dismay as he pushed her away.

His brilliant jade eyes burnt her cheeks scarlet as he

held her on the pyre of his lust and anger. She watched with alarm as the muscles knotted in his jaw as he cried out in impassioned fury, "God, Catherine. Coming near you is like walking on the edge of a volcano. It only takes one unwary step and I'm plunged into the heat. I don't mind admitting that I'll be glad when I'm shut of this situation."

He left her then. With the tears flooding, she finished getting ready as best she could.

Her makeup was on—hiding the ravages, she hoped —when Cleopatra came in, and she was brushing her hair to complete her toilette. Cleopatra always came in at about that time to turn down the bed. Catherine had stopped telling her not to bother. She made her own bed and kept her room tidy, as well as taking it upon herself to do some dusting around the house. It had long since occurred to her that Cleopatra kept the pre-dinner vigil to admire—or criticize, Catherine received as much of one as the other—her choice of dress and to enjoy a gossip session.

"A pretty brush, Miss Catherine." Cleopatra had commented before on how taken she was with the ivory backs and the long elegant handles adorning the mirror and brush set. "For pretty hair," she added. "But where is my lady's pretty smile? You been having a fight with Mister Paul again, you foolish child?"

"I'm too impetuous. I jump into situations without knowing what they're about. He's sick of bailing me out. I'm a nuisance he would be better off without."

"Now what nitwit has been telling you that load of rubbish?"

"Paul has. He says he'll be glad when he gets shut of me."

"What does he know? He's a man, and bless their beautiful hides men sometimes go around like they've got a hole in their heads where their brains should be."

"Now, Cleopatra, that's not fair. You're encouraging me to insult him, and if I do you'll be down on me like a ton of bricks, because no one can say a word against your precious Mister Paul in your hearing."

Cleopatra chuckled cheekily. "Except me. He doesn't really want to see the back of you, honey. He loves you, I'm sure. Maybe he doesn't know it yet."

"That's not true. I wouldn't tell this to anyone else, but I know it's safe with you. I'm not his woman. We're not lovers. Letting people think we are is just a cover. My being here prevents a recurrence of last time's gossip."

"I knows that, just as I knows a lot of things nobody tells me. Seems to me that might have been his reason for having you here in the first place, but it ain't no reason now. Not the way that Zoe creature is chasing him."

"She wants him back," said Catherine.

"She can want until forever, but she won't get him."

"If only I could believe that you were right, Cleopatra, but I know differently. Zoe is so lovely, how can Paul resist her?"

"He's resisting her now, ain't he?"

"Only because he's working flat out and hasn't time for any social life. Once filming is completed, he'll turn to her; you'll see."

"No, Miss Catherine. You got to be wrong. He couldn't tie himself up with a harlot like that, not when a sweet little gal like you is waiting to be picked up. You'd be so good for him, Miss Catherine."

As it was still a little on the early side, Catherine decided to take a stroll in the garden before presenting herself at the poolside for the customary pre-dinner drink. On impulse she walked beyond the garden and followed the path that would take her to the lagoon.

Ever since Paul had led her out to the balcony of their hotel in New Providence to show her her first tropical sunset she had been fascinated by the nightly spectacle, but she had not yet viewed the sunset from the lagoon.

As she stood at the water's edge she sensed another presence. Turning her head she said, "Hi," to Paul.

"Two minds with but a single thought."

"Yes," she said, liking the compatible sound of that, even though she wasn't enamored of the grimness still adhering to his mouth.

"I think I've settled the problem of a stand-in."

"You have?"

"I've sent Jock after Joanna with a message for her to come back."

"Do you think she will?"

"Oh, yes. As a bribe, I've offered terms she can't refuse. An apology from Zoe in front of everyone, and dinner on the town with me when the last shot is in the can and things are back to normal. The dinner date with me will carry the day, of course."

"Undoubtedly," she said, smiling at his supreme arrogance, then realizing he wasn't being arrogant at all but had just made what he thought was a joke. "How are you going to get Zoe to make a public apology?"

"I've also offered her . . . er . . . terms she can't refuse."

"Oh?" Her heart plummeted.

"In return for her making the apology, I have promised not to break her neck."

There was sadness behind her affected laugh as she wondered what he had really offered to bring the temperamental actress to heel.

The sun dropped lower. Blue-pink, blood-red and purple swaths draped to dramatic effect across the clouds. She released a sigh of deep appreciation. She would never tire of watching tropical sunsets. It was over, but by unspoken agreement neither of them moved, choosing to stay and soak up the last remnants of the afterglow. Somewhere in the enchanted dusk a night bird sang; the lagoon glinted with a silvery purple luminosity and was startlingly beautiful.

The never-sleeping wind wound long silky strands of hair across her mouth. Fingers other than her own drew them away to uncover it, but its aching longing was not to be appeased. He made no attempt to kiss her.

Dear, kind-hearted Cleopatra, telling her what she so much wanted to hear, knowing it bore no relation to the truth. If Paul had any feeling for her at all he wouldn't have been able to stop himself from taking her into his arms and crushing her to him for dear life. It would have been impossible for him to hold himself aloof from her in these heavenly surroundings . . . the scent of exotic flowers pervading the senses and the drugging, hypnotic sound of the surf crashing on the reef. Romance was everywhere, even in the poignant ache in her throat, the dangerous unprecedented urges which a short while ago she might have been reluctant to own. Her obsessive longing for Paul . . . she wanted him . . . wanted him to make love to her with an urgency that was unseemly. His nearness tormented her. She wanted him so much.

In that moment she knew that the most beautiful place in the world wasn't paradise. Paradise wasn't a place; it was a state of mind. It was two people in love. When only one person loved, the most beautiful place on earth could be a living hell.

The cast and crew were preparing to depart for home. Paul was staying on to wind things up and would follow in his own time. Catherine wasn't given the option; she was being sent home with the others. He couldn't wait to see the back of her. Well, that suited her. Her one desire, she told herself, was to walk away and never have to see him again.

She was sorry to say goodbye to Cleopatra who, in a comparatively short time, had become her friend. She wished she had a parting gift to give the woman, a token of affection to say how much she'd enjoyed her company and her counsel during those evening gossip sessions. And then she realized that she had the perfect gift in her possession, something Cleopatra greatly admired, her ivory-backed hairbrush set. It didn't matter that it was also precious to her. It was only a possession. A friendship was more precious.

Cleopatra, remembering that Catherine had once told her how she had come by it, said half-protestingly, "But your momma gave this to you."

"She would have liked you, Cleopatra. She would have understood and wanted you to have it."

"Bless you, child."

His jade eyes dull, his whole body drooping with tiredness, Paul had still insisted on accompanying them to the airport, even though one of the members of the crew had promised to keep a fatherly eye on Catherine.

She wanted to say, "You work too hard. Is it worth it? Take time to eat your meals, darling, and go to bed at a reasonable hour." Instead she said, "I hate goodbyes."

"This one won't be for long. I'll be with you in, oh . . . four days at the outside."

If only he meant it. If only he wasn't still saving face in front of the others, who had discreetly moved away to give them a few moments alone together to say their goodbyes, but were still within hearing and seeing distance.

"Do you think you can put a firm clamp on your impulsive nature and stay out of trouble until then?"

"I'll . . . try," she said, speaking 'round a lump in her throat the size of a duck egg, or so it seemed.

"What's Ally's phone number? I'll give her a ring and alert her that you're coming."

She told him and he jotted it down.

"I'll feel better knowing you'll be met."

She had expected him to kiss her, for the benefit of the others, but even so, she was unprepared for the force with which he swept her into his arms. Searing, cherishing, lifting her off the ground, his kiss took every part of her into the custody of his *feigned* caring.

If only it could have been for real. If only he were really this unwilling to let her go.

She boarded the plane blindly, the tears coursing unashamedly, agonizingly, down her cheeks. Someone —the cameraman who'd volunteered to keep an eye on her, she thought—said, "It was like tearing his right arm off to let you go. And you're no better. You two sure have something good going for you!"

Something very good, a good sham . . . on Paul's part, anyway, she thought bitterly.

Paul must have got through to Ally on the telephone, because there she was, waiting for Catherine and waving like mad as the jet touched down.

Catherine couldn't wait to get through the formalities and fall into her friend's arms. "Oh, Ally, it's good to see you. You don't know how good."

More tears, happy tears this time, mingled as affectionate kisses of greeting were exchanged, and then Ally said, "You've got the most gorgeous suntan, but that's the only thing good about you. Haven't you been sleeping properly? You look positively haggard, all eyes and anguish. I'm going to take you home with me and spoil you rotten. I want to hear everything that's happened to you, but can I be very selfish and get my news in first? Because if I don't tell you I'll explode!" Without waiting for consent she charged straight on. "I'm getting married again."

"Oh, Ally, that's marvelous! When?"

"Not too soon. In about six months' time. I want to give proper respect to Ray."

"He wouldn't have wanted you to waste yourself in widowhood, Ally. He would have been overjoyed for you—just as I am. Who's the lucky guy? Anyone I know?"

"You should, but you don't." Ally's face was a mixture of concern and laughter. "Funny you should call him lucky, because that's who he is. Lucky Chance, the author you were supposed to be going out to work for."

"You know about the mix-up? That's a stupid question. If you've met the real author, and got on such friendly terms with him that you're going to marry him, obviously you know. I expect you can guess what happened. At the party, I picked the wrong man."

"Did you?" Ally inquired with more astuteness than she could have imagined. "If your face is anything to go by, I guess that's so. You left the right one for me."

Where did she go from here? Catherine wondered. Ally's forthcoming marriage to her Lucian meant that Allycats would have to be wound up. It had been Ally's brainchild, her baby, and Catherine didn't feel any great sense of loss about that. No, not about that . . .

She spent the next three days telling herself that Paul had merely been talking and that he wouldn't get in touch with her. After all, why should he? She had served her usefulness. He had made his point to Zoe and the rest of the team, and if he did have plans for getting back with Zoe, she herself would only be an encumbrance. But when the phone rang on day three, the sound of his voice seriously impeded the beat of her heart, and she knew that she had been living in expectation of that call.

"I've just got in. Will you meet me for lunch?"

"Where?"

He named a place. She got the feeling he'd picked it out at random. His voice sounded strained. She promised to be there in half an hour. As she put the phone down she realized she'd been impulsive again. Why did she always speak first and think afterward? Would it hurt for her to get things in the right order for once? Thirty minutes, including getting-there time, didn't give her much leeway. She ought to have insisted on at least two hours in which to indulge in a leisurely toilette and choose something really flattering to wear. Ally, who had been the soul of tact and hadn't plied her with one embarrassing or hurtful question, although she must have been burning up with curiosity about what had happened, helped out by calling a cab and assuring Catherine that she looked delicious enough to eat in her hastily donned dress and warm coat. She still wasn't conditioned to the change in climate.

Paul was already installed at a table when she got there. He pulled out a chair for her and she thankfully sank down. Her legs weren't behaving too well.

"Hello, kitten-face," he said, and her heart turned over.

The beard had gone, but the tiredness was even more deeply etched on his face. He looked as though he needed to go to bed for a week.

"I'm sorry about this dreadful place," he apologized. "I couldn't think of anywhere to suggest, although I must know a hundred places—slight exaggeration, but you know what I mean."

It was rather uninspiring, somber colors and apparently indifferent service, because no one was rushing to take their order, but it was beautiful in her eyes because she was with Paul. Get on with it, her heart pleaded. Please say something.

He placed an oblong box on the table. "Your property safely returned to you. Something you've missed perhaps?"

"You mean something I forgot to pack? There's nothing as far as I know."

"Your hairbrush set. The one with the pretty ivory backs. Cleopatra found it after you'd gone. She asked me to act as delivery boy. She said you knew how much she coveted it and she would hate you to think she had stolen it. Cleopatra isn't a thief."

Catherine had given the set to Cleopatra. Cleopatra had invented the story of Catherine's having left it behind to set up a meeting between her and Paul. For one wild, improbable moment she'd thought that Paul had come on his own initiative, that he'd realized he couldn't live without her and had come to claim her. The desolation of knowing that wasn't so was almost more than she could bear.

No, Cleopatra wasn't a thief. She was dear and sweet and misinformed, and Catherine wished she hadn't meddled. After the wonderful surge of hope that had gone through her when Paul phoned, how was she going to sit there and talk normally and not let him know how utterly and irredeemably she loved him?

She couldn't give Cleopatra away, and so she said, "I'm sorry you've been put to the trouble of returning it. Perhaps leaving it was a Freudian slip, because I meant to make a gift of it to Cleopatra. I must get it back to her somehow."

"It was no trouble at all. I was coming to see you in any case."

"You were?"

"Didn't I say so at the airport?"

"I thought that was for the others."

"And that kiss?" he queried. "Whose benefit do you think that was for?"

"The others', just the same. For the sake of appearance."

"I've never cared all that much about what other people think or say."

"But you asked me to stay with you so there wouldn't be a recurrence of the old gossip."

His smile was endearingly sheepish. "I had to say something to keep you under my eye. I must admit that my original reason for wanting you there was to salvage my pride, but then everything changed, and I just wanted you with me. Can you imagine the dilemma I was in when our mutual mix-up came to light? That funny look on your face—shock, horror, indignation—will live forever in my mind. I knew that you meant it when you said you were going home. No way was I going to risk that. By the time filming was finished and I could follow you, you might have met someone else. But I couldn't give you the attention you deserved either. There weren't enough hours in the day to get through what I had to do as it was. I was tied up doing a very exacting job. I couldn't drop everything, go back to the beginning, and court you properly, ideal as that would have been."

"But why would you want to?"

"Can't you guess?"

"Very probably. I'm good at guessing, jumping to conclusions. I've been given strict instructions not to, because it always lands me in dreadful trouble," said Catherine.

"Mm. As I'm the one who gave you those instructions, I suppose I can't grumble. The simple truth is, I had something quite good going for me, but then I spoiled it all by falling in love with you."

"You—what?"

"I fell in love with you."

"And that spoiled it?"

"In a sense. It was a killer situation from the word go. Scruples got in the way, and I don't just mean yours. I was madly attracted to you from the beginning, but when I thought you were on the make, although I wanted you more than I've ever wanted a woman in my life, I fought to resist it. Then, when I found out that it was all a mistake, that you were everything I ever dreamed of finding in a woman, I couldn't take advantage of you. Not to mention that I made the error of giving you my word that I wouldn't lay a finger on you when we were alone."

"A promise which you broke," she reminded him.

"Yes. To my shame, I wasn't very honorable. My feelings sort of piled up on me. Your full and very warm cooperation was my undoing. After seeming to be on intimate terms with you in public, it was hell having to get back into line in private. I couldn't keep my hands off you when we were alone, and I didn't play fair when others were present. I made the most of you, for my own self-indulgence. By that time I didn't give a hoot what they thought. But I cared for you."

The waitress came to take their order. He waited until she had gone and then picked up from where he had left off.

"Walking past your door that night, letting you decide, was the most difficult thing I've ever done in my life. Poor little kitten, you had nothing to draw on, no heavy emotional situations in your past. You didn't know what it was all about. I should have looked after you, not tried to railroad you into something. I shouldn't have let myself get carried away."

"I won't let you take all the blame," said Catherine. "We both got carried away. But I really was coming to your room to say that I couldn't go through with it. I thought the love scene you played with Zoe earlier in the day had got you steamed up, and that you just wanted to work your passions out on me. And then, when I saw Zoe in your room, I thought you wouldn't need me, after all."

"I couldn't get rid of Zoe fast enough. She was getting to be a pain in the neck, but I had the film to complete and she was rather an essential character, so I had to go along with her stupid pretexts and placate her. I don't know what I ever saw in her in the first place. I suppose she filled a purpose, and that's all there was to it. I've never lain awake at night, hollowed out with longing for her as I have for you. I've never been driven to the brink of desperation with desire for her. There were times . . . One occasion stands out in particular, the last time we watched the sunset together. You wouldn't have noticed, but I wanted you so much I didn't dare touch you."

"I noticed," she said brokenly.

"What I'm leading up to is this. Can we start again? Do you think you can bring yourself to cancel out the bad beginning and give me another chance? Give me time to prove how much I love you. Is that too much to ask? And, hopefully, if I'm very lucky, you'll come to love me."

"But I love you already. And *I* hope that you're not going to become too saintly, because I fell in love with you just as you were, and I couldn't bear it if you changed too drastically."

"Are you saying that you're not going to make me wait? You'll marry me at once?" he asked urgently.

"I was right," she said huskily, "when I thought that paradise wasn't a certain place. It's everywhere . . .

could be anywhere . . . even here." She was enchanted by his caring. His words sparkled in her mind like sunbeams. This dull, cold day, these drab surroundings, would always stay golden in her mind. She laughed. "What am I saying, 'even here'? *Especially* here. When I came in just now, it wrung my heart to see how tired you looked. The thought crossed my mind that you needed to go to bed for a week. Can I come with you?"

"Not the traditionally worded acceptance. But, from you, perhaps the predictable one." He took some bills from his wallet, and placed them on the table to cover the food they'd ordered, which hadn't yet arrived. "Food can wait. Let's get out of here," he said thickly. "I'm a *very* tired man."

IT'S YOUR OWN SPECIAL TIME
Contemporary romances for today's women.
Each month, six very special love stories will be yours
from SILHOUETTE. Look for them wherever books are sold
or order now from the coupon below.

$1.50 each

☐ 5 Goforth	☐ 28 Hampson	☐ 54 Beckman	☐ 83 Halston
☐ 6 Stanford	☐ 29 Wildman	☐ 55 LaDame	☐ 84 Vitek
☐ 7 Lewis	☐ 30 Dixon	☐ 56 Trent	☐ 85 John
☐ 8 Beckman	☐ 32 Michaels	☐ 57 John	☐ 86 Adams
☐ 9 Wilson	☐ 33 Vitek	☐ 58 Stanford	☐ 87 Michaels
☐ 10 Caine	☐ 34 John	☐ 59 Vernon	☐ 88 Stanford
☐ 11 Vernon	☐ 35 Stanford	☐ 60 Hill	☐ 89 James
☐ 17 John	☐ 38 Browning	☐ 61 Michaels	☐ 90 Major
☐ 19 Thornton	☐ 39 Sinclair	☐ 62 Halston	☐ 92 McKay
☐ 20 Fulford	☐ 46 Stanford	☐ 63 Brent	☐ 93 Browning
☐ 22 Stephens	☐ 47 Vitek	☐ 71 Ripy	☐ 94 Hampson
☐ 23 Edwards	☐ 48 Wildman	☐ 73 Browning	☐ 95 Wisdom
☐ 24 Healy	☐ 49 Wisdom	☐ 76 Hardy	☐ 96 Beckman
☐ 25 Stanford	☐ 50 Scott	☐ 78 Oliver	☐ 97 Clay
☐ 26 Hastings	☐ 52 Hampson	☐ 81 Roberts	☐ 98 St. George
☐ 27 Hampson	☐ 53 Browning	☐ 82 Dailey	☐ 99 Camp

$1.75 each

☐ 100 Stanford	☐ 114 Michaels	☐ 128 Hampson	☐ 143 Roberts
☐ 101 Hardy	☐ 115 John	☐ 129 Converse	☐ 144 Goforth
☐ 102 Hastings	☐ 116 Lindley	☐ 130 Hardy	☐ 145 Hope
☐ 103 Cork	☐ 117 Scott	☐ 131 Stanford	☐ 146 Michaels
☐ 104 Vitek	☐ 118 Dailey	☐ 132 Wisdom	☐ 147 Hampson
☐ 105 Eden	☐ 119 Hampson	☐ 133 Rowe	☐ 148 Cork
☐ 106 Dailey	☐ 120 Carroll	☐ 134 Charles	☐ 149 Saunders
☐ 107 Bright	☐ 121 Langan	☐ 135 Logan	☐ 150 Major
☐ 108 Hampson	☐ 122 Scofield	☐ 136 Hampson	☐ 151 Hampson
☐ 109 Vernon	☐ 123 Sinclair	☐ 137 Hunter	☐ 152 Halston
☐ 110 Trent	☐ 124 Beckman	☐ 138 Wilson	☐ 153 Dailey
☐ 111 South	☐ 125 Bright	☐ 139 Vitek	☐ 154 Beckman
☐ 112 Stanford	☐ 126 St. George	☐ 140 Erskine	☐ 155 Hampson
☐ 113 Browning	☐ 127 Roberts	☐ 142 Browning	☐ 156 Sawyer

$1.75 each

- [ ] 157 Vitek
- [ ] 158 Reynolds
- [ ] 159 Tracy
- [ ] 160 Hampson
- [ ] 161 Trent
- [ ] 162 Ashby
- [ ] 163 Roberts
- [ ] 164 Browning
- [ ] 165 Young
- [ ] 166 Wisdom
- [ ] 167 Hunter
- [ ] 168 Carr
- [ ] 169 Scott

- [ ] 170 Ripy
- [ ] 171 Hill
- [ ] 172 Browning
- [ ] 173 Camp
- [ ] 174 Sinclair
- [ ] 175 Jarrett
- [ ] 176 Vitek
- [ ] 177 Dailey
- [ ] 178 Hampson
- [ ] 179 Beckman
- [ ] 180 Roberts
- [ ] 181 Terrill
- [ ] 182 Clay

- [ ] 183 Stanley
- [ ] 184 Hardy
- [ ] 185 Hampson
- [ ] 186 Howard
- [ ] 187 Scott
- [ ] 188 Cork
- [ ] 189 Stephens
- [ ] 190 Hampson
- [ ] 191 Browning
- [ ] 192 John
- [ ] 193 Trent
- [ ] 194 Barry
- [ ] 195 Dailey

- [ ] 196 Hampson
- [ ] 197 Summers
- [ ] 198 Hunter
- [ ] 199 Roberts
- [ ] 200 Lloyd
- [ ] 201 Starr
- [ ] 202 Hampson
- [ ] 203 Browning
- [ ] 204 Carroll
- [ ] 205 Maxam
- [ ] 206 Manning
- [ ] 207 Windham

$1.95 each

- [ ] 208 Halston
- [ ] 209 LaDame
- [ ] 210 Eden
- [ ] 211 Walters
- [ ] 212 Young

- [ ] 213 Dailey
- [ ] 214 Hampson
- [ ] 215 Roberts
- [ ] 216 Saunders
- [ ] 217 Vitek

- [ ] 218 Hunter
- [ ] 219 Cork
- [ ] 220 Hampson
- [ ] 221 Browning
- [ ] 222 Carroll

- [ ] 223 Summers
- [ ] 224 Langan
- [ ] 225 St. George

___#226 SWEET SECOND LOVE, Hampson

___#227 FORBIDDEN AFFAIR, Beckman

___#228 DANCE AT YOUR WEDDING, King

___#229 FOR ERIC'S SAKE, Thornton

___#230 IVORY INNOCENCE, Stevens

___#231 WESTERN MAN, Dailey

___#232 SPELL OF THE ISLAND, Hampson

___#233 EDGE OF PARADISE, Vernon

___#234 NEXT YEAR'S BLONDE, Smith

___#235 NO EASY CONQUEST, James

___#236 LOST IN LOVE, Maxam

___#237 WINTER PROMISE, Wilson

SILHOUETTE BOOKS, Department SB/1

1230 Avenue of the Americas
New York, NY 10020

Please send me the books I have checked above. I am enclosing $_____
(please add 50¢ to cover postage and handling. NYS and NYC residents please
add appropriate sales tax). Send check or money order—no cash or C.O.D.'s
please. Allow six weeks for delivery.

NAME _____

ADDRESS _____

CITY _____ STATE/ZIP _____

6 brand new Silhouette Special Editions yours for 15 days–Free!

For the reader who wants more…more story…more detail and description…more realism…and more romance…in paperback originals, 1/3 longer than our regular Silhouette Romances. Love lingers longer in new Silhouette Special Editions. Love weaves an intricate, provocative path in a third more pages than you have just enjoyed. It is love as you have always wanted it to be—and more —intriguingly depicted by your favorite Silhouette authors in the inimitable Silhouette style.

15-Day Free Trial Offer

We will send you 6 new Silhouette Special Editions to keep for 15 days absolutely free! If you decide not to keep them, send them back to us, you pay nothing. But if you enjoy them as much as we think you will, keep them and pay the invoice enclosed with your trial shipment. You will then automatically become a member of the Special Edition Book Club and receive 6 more romances every month. There is no minimum number of books to buy and you can cancel at any time.